Glass

"A darkly delicious ex        t,
*Dreams Under Glass* is both a coming-of-age novel and a horror story about gluttony, greed, and art. Szilágyi binds the spell with confectionary precision and a collector's sense of wonder and ceaseless want. This book rattles with its refraction of a world in which telling the truth might be the most difficult art."

—Nancy Jooyoun Kim, *New York Times* bestselling author of *The Last Story of Mina Lee*

"It's Szilágyi doing what she does best: sublime language laced with stunningly original imagery and mordant wit."

—Kris Waldherr, bestselling author of *The Lost History of Dreams* and *Unnatural Creatures*

"Szilágyi's sharp, wry prose captures millennial ennui and ambition alike in this sometimes dark, sometimes electric, completely fascinating novel."

—Sonora Jha, author of *Foreign* and *How to Raise a Feminist Son*

"*Dreams Under Glass*...is a broken glass eye gazing up at you while you stand in cheap heels for too long around people who will never love you."

—Corinne Manning, author of *We Had No Rules*

# Dreams Under Glass

**Also by Anca L. Szilágyi**

*Daughters of the Air*

# Dreams Under Glass

### A Novel

by Anca L. Szilágyi

## LANTERNFISH PRESS
Philadelphia

Lanternfish Press
21 S. 11th Street, Office #404
Philadelphia, PA 19107
lanternfishpress.com

Cover Design: Kimberly Glyder
Cover Art: Nichole DeMent

Printed in the United States of America.
26 25 24 23 22    1 2 3 4 5

Library of Congress Control Number: 2021944828
Print ISBN: 978-1-941360-67-5
Digital ISBN: 978-1-941360-68-2

For my family

# Chapter One

THE BLACK CAR spat Binnie out at 53rd and Third. The lawyer she was riding with had lost his casino bankruptcy trial, big time, and wore a pitiful countenance. She'd almost tried to put him out of his misery with a kiss. Had he noticed it was happening? She replayed in her mind the way she'd leaned slightly forward toward his sorry face and loosened tie. He could probably tell. Well. That was embarrassing.

Mistakes: the price of knowledge. She'd pick up her paycheck and move on with her Friday night. The sun had already set, and she'd made plans while at the Newark stop on the Acela to meet her friend Gary for dinner. Romance had not been part of their history, although lately their relationship hummed with a subtle electric charge. They'd weathered several stupid relationships together, like hers with a boy who now squatted in Detroit hoping to be the next Banksy and his with a girl who aspired to be a diplomat and found Gary's Iraqi-Jewish lineage titillating. Now they were, for the first time in their five-year friendship, both single.

The driver deposited her rolly bag on the sidewalk. The lawyer muttered from inside the car, "See ya Monday." Her bag went *tha-thunk tha-thunk* as her clearance-rack heels clacked down the sidewalk.

Gary waited for her beneath the pink granite pillars of the Lipstick Building, cheeks rosy from the first chill of fall, fists thrust into charcoal jacket pockets, a black knit cap hiding his brown curls. When he saw Binnie, he lifted his head from its natural melancholic tilt and smiled. Still wound up from the trial, the loss, the pitiful lawyer, a harshness balled up in her chest, she said, "You could've waited in the lobby."

His dark eyelashes brushed up against his wire-rim glasses. He said, "I've had my daily allotment of recycled air." She softened and they hugged, their usual platonic hips-angled-away-from-each-other hug.

"Want to come up?"

The security guard took Gary's ID. The security arm at the gate buzzed open. Binnie imagined an art project using robotic arms. Gatekeepers, access, automation. Articulated arms moving like octopi. But what did she know about robots? *Stick to the basics, honey.*

On a huge sign by the elevator bank, the law firm Latham & Watkins advertised its presence in the building, but there were countless other mysterious tenants—investment firms and hedge funds and what-not. Celebrity divorce lawyers. Binnie had shared the elevator with Uma Thurman once, a story which her father found thrilling; he claimed she looked like her. *Hardly,* she'd said. *Let's start with how short I am, how frizzy my brittle hair, how frail my bird bones.* The firm she worked for—Capra Zaiman Baxter, or CZB—was nothing fancy compared to Latham & Watkins or Uma Thurman's divorce attorney. A "boutique" (read: scrappy) firm with three partners, one full-time associate Binnie privately dubbed "the Zombie," a rotating cast of part-time contract attorneys, and underlings like Binnie.

The elevator rocketed upward. Gary and Binnie rode in silence, eyes glued to the TV screen. On the news ticker, Lehman Brothers was kaput, its bankruptcy announced that Monday. Sarah Palin, the folksy, self-proclaimed "maverick" governor of Alaska, performed her hockey-mom, pitbull-with-lipstick shtick. And Stephen Hawking unveiled something called a "Corpus Clock," a "time eater."

Before Binnie could ask Gary if he remembered that old Robin Williams movie about yuppicide, the doors slid open with a *ding* and her phone buzzed.

*Dinner tonight?*

"Mind if Ellen joins us?"

Deadpan, Gary said sure. Between the gold plastic gift card Baxter had given her in the car ("Good job," he'd murmured, looking like he wanted to die) and the impending paycheck fattened from overtime, Binnie was feeling celebratory. She'd been avoiding Ellen, for many reasons, but chiefly because Ellen had no clue how expensive her taste was and Binnie hated it when she offered to pay.

*Park Slope? Al Di La?*

Binnie's thumb hesitated over the keys as she expelled a long sigh. *Sure. I got a bonus! My treat.* She regretted this immediately but would stick to it. *Gary's coming too.*

*Fun.*

Behind the reception desk, *Namaste* somersaulted languidly across Madeline's screen, a whorl of thin neon letters.

Binnie tiptoed into Beatrice's cubicle, unsure why she felt as if she were sneaking around, trespassing, even though Beatrice had given her specific instructions. She spun the dial on the petty cash box's combination lock and found her check while Gary wandered into the conference room to admire the view.

Beneath her check was one of Rick's pay stubs. Rick, the senior paralegal, the red-haired boy her age who wore bow ties to work and lorded his seniority over her. When she'd asked, naively, why the casino bankruptcy trial was happening in Delaware, he'd said, "Because it's corporate America's Wild Wild West," and extended his thumb and pointer finger into the shape of a gun. Pointed it at Binnie's head. Said in a baby voice, "Pow!"

"Hey," Beatrice had warned, voice lowered to a contralto. "No imaginary shootings in the workplace."

"Didja know I'm a card-carrying member of the NRA?" Rick cackled, pulling a card out of his wallet and waggling it in Beatrice's face.

"Ew." Her manicured hands flew up; her summer braids swayed. "Get that thing out of here, you creep."

It was then that the "Wild Wild Wilmington" diorama occurred to Binnie: a vast wasteland littered with hundreds of tumbleweed-like balls of crumpled-up credit card offers. Small print pasted in the background, like the vintage maps of Florence lining Joseph Cornell's "Medici Slot Machine", or better yet the astronomical maps in his night sky series. Redacting the text with a thick black marker, she'd form clouds and constellations of legalese loopholes. Instead of Andromeda or Casseopeia longing for the star-studded expanse outside the windows of white, shoe-box-sized hotel rooms, she'd have a cowboy in the open air, wielding a lasso. And yet, of course, the open air would still be inside a box. "Freedom" still a trap.

Now Binnie goggled at how much Rick made. A pain sunk into her sternum. Did Beatrice leave the stub in there on purpose? Did Rick? Why? The difference was staggering. He made nearly twice as much as she did. Binnie was surprised at how much it hurt, physically pained her, burned her cheeks. How much did Madeline make? And how much did Beatrice make? How long would it take her to make as much as Rick? How much faster would a salary like his clear a student loan debt like hers? And he was so smug, Rick. Like he knew how to get away with—living. Like he was playing the game he'd been trained to play since birth and she didn't even know which game pieces went where: she just gawped at them like a rube.

At her job interview, silver-haired Capra had asked in his radio broadcaster voice what salary she had in mind.

Binnie, having diligently studied GetThatJob.com, turned it around on him. "What did *you* have in mind?"

Capra narrowed his eyes, a hint of the Bronx peeping out. "I asked you first."

Binnie gulped. "Based on my research, thirty to thirty-five?"

He jotted that on her resume, pleased.

"That's very reasonable, Binnie. Some people get the wrong idea. Let's have you meet Zaiman." She'd immediately wondered if she should have asked for more. The only thing Zaiman wanted to know was how she got a 4.0, but she didn't want to snap that she got an A+ in Underwater Basketweaving. To her semi-coherent chatter about diligence, he said, "I give up," and the interview was over. Baxter didn't interview Binnie at all. Later she'd assume they left him out because his tendency toward indecision would have mucked up how speedily they wished to move.

From the threshold to the conference room, Gary asked, "What's wrong?"

"What? Nothing."

Gary lowered his head to catch Binnie's gaze. "Sure?" Her palms were sweating. She managed a quasi-genuine grin. "Get a load of this view."

The East River glimmered. All of Queens expanded in the night, an endless shimmering evening gown. "Pretty fantastic."

"You get this view every day?"

"I guess. Not much time to take it in."

"You know what I have a view of?"

"I know. A gray cubicle wall." She glanced outside but only saw the innards of the office reflected in the window. "Sorry."

"Try to take a minute out of each day and just *look* at that."

She tried harder to appreciate the view, but an angry little goblin niggled in her ear, an evil Keebler elf, reminiscent of Rick. She hadn't been invited to the trial because she was competent. She'd been invited because she was cheap. She pressed her forehead to the cold glass until the prickly feeling subsided. *What do you care,* she thought over and over again. *This is just a day job. Not art.*

The meat grinder, a floor-to-ceiling subway turnstile with peeling black paint, whined as they passed through, Binnie's rolly bag awkward in the mix. On the crowded train, their bodies swayed together, hugging the same pole.

"Aren't you exhausted?"

"Wired." She forced a smile. "Hungry."

"I learned a new trick at work today! Y'know how they've got me calling ladies in Tennessee hawking makeup kits? I'm putting on a drawl. *Ma'am, this'll go great with your beautiful blue eyes.*"

"Wait, but how do you know their eye color?"

"Doesn't matter. Works like magic."

"You're a sales genius."

At the summer internship where they met, Gary had sold record numbers of *Samba Fever!* to a school district in Oregon when his boss was in Hawaii for a week.

"Pure luck," he'd said, ever humble.

His boss gave him a free copy of *Samba Fever! Disco Remix* and kept the commission. Technically, the place was a nonprofit. They got Metrocards, ten dollars a day for lunch, and "experience."

Gary hadn't planned on working in a call center again *after* graduation. But he graduated in 2003 in a job market of...nothing. And like Binnie, he was deeply in debt, more so because he'd funded all four years of his education entirely with loans. His first job out of school was cold-call fundraising to cure a rare and horrible degenerative disease. It paid $8.50 per hour and his voice cracked and frazzled over stories of children atrophying in their beds. Selling wine and cosmetics kept him above water, more or less, and the content of his spiel no longer crushed him."So where are we going again?"

Binnie grimaced. "Al Di La. My treat."

"Mama Warbucks."

Leaning toward Gary on the subway pole, she said, "I think we'll be spared Ellen's luvah."

"Mr. Where Can I Find the Next Rothko?"

"The same."

Ellen had a place on the Upper West Side but lately she'd been living with a guy who'd strolled into the West Chelsea art gallery where she worked seeking an investment opportunity. A bold color field, perhaps in hues of saffron or cobalt, to make the white brick of his refurbished Prospect Heights brownstone pop. When Binnie met him, he wore his sunglasses behind his head. She'd been surprised Ellen was okay with this fashion choice. But he'd played rugby in college, Ellen said, and his thick-necked vitality evened things out for her.

The hostess offered to take Binnie's suitcase, but she refused, worried she'd forget it, and wove through the restaurant behind Gary, the wheels catching against chair legs. "Sorry," she said to annoyed diners, hating herself.

The blue glow of Ellen's smartphone, mixed with candlelight, rendered her skin luminous, like a Renoir painting. Her expression suggested faint amusement as she calmly tapped away at an epic text message. She always embodied composure. She always synced with her surroundings. In college, Binnie had always been passed over for the awards which professors mysteriously bestowed upon certain anointed peers. Maybe Ellen's inborn knowledge of societal expectations (no one really works nine to five; schmoozing takes charm, class, quick thinking, and knowing how to make an exit) was part of what keyed her in to the opportunities that appeared before her on a silver platter. Maybe it didn't hurt that a room at the library where Binnie had worked was named after Ellen's grandma.

Ellen brightened at Binnie and Gary's arrival, and she hugged them each in that way she had where Binnie could never tell if it was genuine. A strong hug, but a beat too long. Like it wasn't really about the affection but the performance of it.

The dark-eyed sommelier and Ellen shared a knowing twinkle; she ordered a red wine from the foothills of Vesuvius. He slow-winked and retreated.

Ellen balanced her chin on interlaced fingers and smiled at Binnie. *You now have my full attention.* She projected warmth, an eagerness to listen carefully that had, over the years, drawn Binnie out of her shell. "So, how was the trial? You must have made a shit-ton in overtime."

*Shit-ton* was new to Ellen's vocabulary. Binnie guessed it was the boyfriend's addition. The condescension made Binnie frown.

"Define shit-ton."

The sommelier presented the volcanic wine to Ellen, popped the cork.

"You'll appreciate the fig and spice," he said. Ellen swirled, sniffed, sipped. Nodded.

As the sommelier faded into the scenery, Gary said, "Better watch out, you're gonna get used to all that money."

He'd said this before. A painful reminder of what she had intended to do but so far was failing at. Save money; get ready for the day when she could focus more intently on making art. She bristled, but then he cocked his head to the side in that gentle way that made Binnie want to hug him. He'd been the first person she told about the paralegal job. She didn't want to give anyone else the satisfaction of hearing that she had, in a way, given up her wacky pursuit of art in an attempt to make an actual living, though it was a living that wasn't grandiose enough to make anyone jealous.

"It's not really that much," said Binnie. Ellen focused intently on the menu. Binnie swirled her wine, picturing glowing lava flows, succulent black grapes fertilized with ash.

She'd told herself the job was a temporary measure—
the unpredictability of working for Gerta had become
intolerable—and that she'd return, imminently, to
her art. But in a fit of rage the night before the trip to
Delaware, she'd swept all the dusty materials from her
work table into the trash: a rubber octopus, a shellacked
clump of strawberry Nerds, a spigot, a ballet shoe. She'd
arranged and rearranged again and again, had struggled
with this assemblage for weeks and for what? It signified
nothing.

Ellen and Gary had never actually seen Binnie's work.
They only knew that their friend was toiling away at
something artsy. The last person she'd showed her work
to was Professor Lewis, her favorite art history professor
in college: a stout woman who slicked her hair back into
a severe bun, but whom Harry Caray glasses rendered
approachable. Professor Lewis taught mid-century
American art, had been the one to introduce Binnie to
Joseph Cornell, the first artist that made Binnie think:
you can do *that*? Toward the end of her last semester, after
the public exhibition of senior projects, which Binnie
had found mortifying—she had taken a last-minute risk,
botched the work, and skipped the party, never asked
Ellen if she'd gone, if she'd seen her stuff—she sheepishly
brought a Cornell-inspired assemblage to Professor Lewis
during office hours. It was not part of her senior project
but something she viewed as private. It was supposed to
be a moonscape, a kind of terrarium filled with gray dirt
and faintly glimmering white pebbles and a sprinkling of
red star-shaped glitter. Professor Lewis pursed her lips at

it, expressed puzzlement. Cooed as if Binnie were a four-year-old presenting her first scribbles, smeared in feces on the wall. The professor had barely remembered her to begin with, despite the college being small, and *this* would be her lasting impression. After that, Binnie abstained from showing her work to most people. She wanted to give it time to mature, perhaps five to ten years. But developing a forceful vision had been impossible on a diet of canned tuna and pilfered oyster crackers.

Binnie was terrified of Ellen's keen critical eye. Ellen viewed life in New York as some kind of extension of an honors seminar, a place to spout opinions, knowledge, and political tracts with supreme confidence and in a loud voice, always ready to follow up with emphatic disagreement. It didn't matter what anyone said. The point was to find an angle and disagree.

Binnie stared at the stem of her glass. Behind it, through the window, the other Fifth Avenue, that of gentrified Brooklyn and not the calcified aristocracy of Manhattan, blurred. *You fucking fuck. What are you doing with your life, making copies?* She sipped her wine. A tiny, sour sip.

"Wait," said Ellen, "a toast!"

Three globular glasses clinked, the burgundy-colored wine glinting against the table's tea lights. Ellen swirled hers again, more dramatically now, sniffed at it lengthily, and slurped.

Binnie snorted. "Ellen."

A toothy smile flashed across her friend's face. "Really though. How are you liking the job?"

"It's fine." Binnie set her glass down.

"You gonna come in to the gallery sometime soon? I can get you started on your own baby collection. I'll point you to the up-and-coming ingénues."

Binnie broke a breadstick and chucked the blunt end at Ellen's chest, surprising herself with the impulsive gesture. Crumbs bounced off Ellen's raw silk chemise. Binnie had meant to be playful but the throw was a tad more violent than she'd intended. She glanced around the genteel restaurant, feeling childish.

"Aw. Behave."

Binnie tittered.

"Ladies, ladies, please. I know you both want me but you have to coexist."

Ellen said, "Ha."

Binnie asked about an email forwarded to her from the gallery while she toiled late one night in the Wilmington hotel room, editing video clips of depositions for the trial. "What's with this booze, bubbles, Basel babies thing?"

"Alexis will be in an acquisitive mood. You should come. Mention your work."

"Oh jeez," said Binnie, gulping at wine. "Right."

"I'll help you sharpen your pitch," Gary said.

A plate of grilled octopus and calamari, peppered with tiny olives glistening in a fine sheen of olive oil and flecked with fresh herbs, floated to their table, mercifully halting the conversation. The tiny arms curled around olives, grasping. How little they resembled the cartoonish red rubber octopus still sitting at the bottom of Binnie's wastebasket. Stabbing one of the tentacled pieces with her fork, she tasted a hint of vinegar and chewed and chewed and chewed on its forbidden flesh.

❖ ❖ ❖

They parted ways, Ellen to her "lover's" abode, Gary to the three-bedroom walkup he shared with five roommates above a toy store on Seventh Avenue. Binnie hopped on the R to Court Street, to the unicorn that was her late Aunt Ruby's rent-controlled apartment.

Despite the short ride, she fell asleep on the train, leaden head bobbing toward the annoyed woman beside her, who scooted away with her toddler. What was that kid doing up so late? The dark bags under the woman's eyes were a fright.

To stay awake, Binnie calculated the evening's expenses: $16 for the octopus primi, $20 for Gary's squid ink spaghetti, $30 for Ellen's braised rabbit, and, because she intentionally ordered last, $12 for her own beet-ricotta ravioli. Plus the $30 Lacryma Christi, a $12 pistachio semi-freddo that Ellen proclaimed better than heroin (not that she'd know), tax, tip...she wanted to cry. Mama Warbucks. She was an idiot.

She read all the subway ads: divorce, bankruptcy, personal injury lawyers; Captain Morgan's Spiced Rum; a public service announcement on how to be a good father; 1-800-ENGLISH; Lose or Gain 40 Pounds in 40 Days; Dr. Zizmore's proclamation against eczema, acne, psoriasis; a clinic promising relief of hemorrhoids, fibroids, erectile dysfunction, and hammertoes, all in the same place.

The train lurched, stopped. The engine hissed. Binnie popped awake. This is it, she thought. This train's dead. This old tunnel's collapsing. She looked up as if to read an explanation in the loudspeaker. Simultaneously, the lights cut. A static-garbled announcement said, *Maggots up ahead.* No. *Traffic,* Binnie. *Traffic.*

A man on the other end of the car said, "Stupidassmuthafuckas."

Got that right, thought Binnie. She leaned forward, elbows to knees. Cricked her neck. As the seconds wore on, she thought perhaps that the conductor had lied, there was no traffic, and she would die underground, sweaty and alone. This was a thought she'd had many times in the seven years since 9/11, whenever stalled in a train tunnel. If a bridge collapsed with her on it, she might be in a car with someone she knew, or close enough to a cabbie to hold his hand as they fell into the water. He'd peer deep into her eyes and their palms would squeeze together just before impact. Down in a subway tunnel it seemed less appropriate to edge closer to a stranger if doom seemed imminent. Especially the stranger she'd fallen asleep on. At least imminent death meant not returning to work! Ha ha!

The toddler shrieked. His mother hushed him. The train rolled backwards, then forward. Soon, they slid into her station. With a sigh, Binnie hoisted herself from the seat. The doors *beee-booooped* behind her. The walk home reawakened her, made her punchy. How easy everyone else at the office had it, she thought. Baxter drove in from Chappaqua in an Escalade with heated leather seats. Capra and Zaiman strolled into work on foot from well-appointed digs with views of the East River. Beatrice and Rick had quick, easy commutes along the 4/5, Beatrice to East Harlem, Rick to the Lower East Side. While Binnie clunked along to Brooklyn dragging a suitcase. Her heels ground into the pavement among slick red leaves illuminated by yellow street lamps.

Home, she kicked off her shoes, peeled off her office clothes. Her stomach rumbled. She stood before the open fridge in her underwear. It was a howling wasteland: a half-eaten cup of yogurt and a half-eaten can of tuna, both protected by tiny squares of Saran wrap, the yogurt dotted with blue and the tuna crusty. In Aunt Ruby's final days, when her mother finally learned how far gone she was, the fridge had been taped shut, full of spoiled lunch meats and whipped-cream Jell-o molds. A pot roast turned gray-green. Binnie slammed the door shut.

In the living room, she stared at her work table. The reason for her existence. The reason she was now at this crappy job, where no one knew a thing about her or cared, where she didn't have time to think about her art. Her trashed assemblage remained in the waste basket, the rubber octopus's googly eye wide with despair. In a low and plodding Eeyore voice, the counterfeit sea creature said: *Pleeeeease, Binnie. Doooon't forsake meeeee.*

She thought of Ruby checking under the bed for monsters and shuddered.

"Sorry, guy. Murder your darlings."

At the corner of the ravaged work table, one object remained: Ruby's cut-glass perfume bottle, circa 1949.

Binnie circled the room once to calm herself before even touching it. Flinging open a window, she inhaled the autumnal night air wafting in from the yards of houses behind her apartment building. Gingko, oak, locust trees shedding their leaves. She poked the mosquito screen. Faint black dust, which drifted in from the Brooklyn-Queens Expressway, smeared onto her finger pad. She sighed, absently wiped the dirt on her pale thigh. Back at the table, she cradled the glass notches of the perfume bottle. Breathed. Sniffed at the relic from a more glamorous time. Rose, jasmine, cedar, musk. The satiny pink tassel tickled her nose.

She locked the window and burrowed into bed, pulling the covers over her face.

Stripes of sunshine shot through the fire escape, warming Binnie's face. She hauled herself awake. Glanced guiltily at her work table, empty but for Ruby's perfume bottle. Light refracted through its cut glass. Eyelids heavy, she dragged herself to the kitchen, numbly prepared a pot of coffee, shuffled back to the table, and sank to the floor, as if kneeling before an altar.

Under the table was a box of materials. She dumped it on the parquet: maple and gingko leaves, old boxes of stale fruit candy, dried peonies, warped copies of *National Geographic*, and crumpled wrapping paper. Cutouts of Glenda the Good Witch, Maria Callas, Groucho Marx, Vladimir Putin, the Marlboro Man, and Bella Lugosi. A green glass electrical conduit, a burgundy Christmas ornament, a crystal ball, a dismantled Swan Lake music box, a Victorian skeleton key. A magnifying glass, scissors, tweezers, shellac, laundry clips, an array of glues.

She tried to make sense of the heap. Sipped coffee and stared in the dead silence of the morning and shivered. The silence didn't feel pregnant. It felt unnervingly sterile.

A crackling jazz record didn't help. She switched on NPR, so quiet that the anchors only murmured warm sounds. No good. The soothing noise poorly covered the void. She was a fool for even considering Ellen's idea.

Already exhausted, she flopped on the sofa. At one point in college, before she found out she would inherit Aunt Ruby's lease, she'd imagined her adult life in New York would involve finding roommates to share a loft in East Bushwick and then making weird little dioramas that would catch the eye of someone influential (*who? someone!*). Kind of like a starlet in a soda shop but different. She'd be discovered by someone who would find her art *unforgettable*. Over time, her art would get better and better until it fetched enough money to live on.

She'd mentioned finding a place in Bushwick to her mother, who'd frowned and said, "Aren't there roving packs of wild dogs there?" (A 1970s story she'd heard from a friend.) And now Binnie lay on Ruby's floral brocade sofa, the kind you would expect to see a plastic slipcover on. She closed her eyes and wished for a television. Maybe she would go to Target one of these days and just get one. But then she'd have to pay for cable too. Lightly, she slapped herself six times on the cheeks. Do. Not. Get. Used. To. Money.

Pigeons fluttered on and off her windowsill. Her flip phone glowed red and buh-buh-buh-BAH-buhhed. She let it buzz a few more times before finally picking up.

"Binnie, honey," said her mother. "We haven't seen you in a month. How are you doing?" Clickty, click.

Binnie imagined her mother fiddling with those clip-on turquoise earrings she loved. "Sorry, Mom. I've been busy. And tired."

"Will you come over for dinner tonight? If it's not too much for you. Your father would love to see you."

It seemed silly to ask if it would be too much. Her parents didn't live out of town. They lived in Kensington. It was one transfer on the subway, although one transfer could really make a thirty-minute trip an expedition.

*Your father would love to see you.*

In a flat voice, Binnie said, "It's not too much trouble. Sorry I've been quiet, I was just in Delaware for two weeks, and there was all the trial prep."

"Of course, honey, we know you're busy. I bet they're working you to the bone. So you'll come and have a bite and we'll hear all about it?"

"Yeah, I'll be there. 6?"

"Sure, whenever you like, sweetie. Just as long as we're done eating in time for *Mystery*."

On the way to the subway, Binnie stopped at the florist and bought her mother an autumnal bouquet, slender branches dotted with smooth red berries. She never bought her mother flowers, which made her feel like a bad daughter, but it was because her mother said she was allergic. These berries were probably okay. Aunt Ruby used to bring snapdragons or gladiolas whenever she came over for dinner, which was a long time ago, and her mother would always mutter "oh dear" and try not to cry at the dinner table.

Up the four flights to their Ocean Parkway co-op, the smells alternated between cabbage soup and sauerkraut and something else—the strange scent of caraway seeds and the solid, homey aroma of boiled potato. Binnie's mother greeted her with familial enthusiasm usually only seen at major holidays, kissing her cheeks and beaming at the bouquet of berried branches before pulling her inside, where it smelled of burnt beans and baked yams.

"Sorry," her father said. "I let your mother cook."

Arlene's smile faded. "You're a little pale. Are you eating enough? How are those lawyers treating you?"

"Fine, Mom."

"Let me nuke those tuna steaks we got in the freezer," her father said. "The girl needs protein."

Her mother clucked her tongue and shook her head.

"We weren't planning on fish tonight, but your father's right."

"Just a few minutes in the nuker, then I'll sear 'em real nice. How's that?"

"And what are you doing wearing heels on a Sunday? What is this? Church? You'll ruin your feet. Not to mention varicose veins."

Binnie slipped off her heels. "I'm trying to get used to wearing them more often. I don't want to look like a kid playing dress-up." She could solder them onto her feet, she thought. Turn into a satyr. Arlene stroked Binnie's cheek with her thumb. The imagined satyr deflated; the air zipped right out of it.

Albert chuckled and padded into the kitchen in his slippers. They'd had Binnie late. Arlene's hair, cropped short, shone silvery gray. Her father sported a round bald head. In a way they seemed more and more like grandparents. Binnie was beginning to feel protective of them.

At the circular wooden table that had been in the small family her whole life, they ate microwaved-and-seared tuna and burnt navy beans and toast and drank tap water.

"So what's with this trial?" asked Albert.

"I probably can't talk about it." She didn't want to talk about the fourteen-hour days, the abject greed of both sides, clients and attorneys alike, the pointlessness, the fact that the judge and jury had used their precious brain power on this litigation. The disgust she felt in herself for feeling disappointed that they lost.

"Top secret, eh?" He smiled a dreamy smile, eyes half-closed.

Binnie leaned in and nodded. If she could be assured invincibility, he probably would've loved for Binnie to be in the CIA or the MI-5. Paralegaling seemed like a semi-thrilling second choice for him, as long as she cut out the boring details. The art, he didn't get. The few pieces she'd shown him, when he'd come over to fix a leak, say, that the super had ignored, were "interesting." Except for the cannibalized book ones. Then he'd say, "I don't care for it, personally."

"Well, everyone's so glad you're in a stable situation," said Arlene. Binnie cringed. "Do you like it?"

"I guess I like it enough."

"Maybe you'll read that LSATs book I gave you."

"Uh, maybe."

"You know you can do art on the side. Everyone has hobbies."

Her face tightened. Sometimes she wondered if part of her motivation to keep pursuing art might be spite. *That's it*, Arlene had said on the phone the middle of Binnie's sophomore year before pulling her financial support. There'd been the silence. Then: *click*.

"I declared my major," she'd said at the beginning of that fateful conversation. The snow outside bright.

"Oh, really?"

"Do tell," said Albert, also on the line.

"Well. Art."

"Art?" Arlene sounded skeptical. "Like art history?"

"No." Her finger traced a groove in the cinderblock dorm wall. "Like making art."

"She's joking, Al, right? I'm not getting the joke?"

"Let her talk," he said. "Binnie. Why art."

"This is my passion. You said find something I love. I want to make things."

"Why not design." His voice quiet. She knew he wouldn't say carpentry. He'd lost a finger.

"At least with art history you could work in a museum. I don't know what kind of prospects you'd have though. Binnie, you really need to reconsider. You need something more—general. More practical."

"I've made my decision. I don't understand why you're saying to change it."

"Binnie, please get real." Her father receded into the background and remained silent during the tuition ultimatum. She wasn't sure if he was standing beside Arlene for that or had gone off to hide in the bathroom. *That's it.* Click.

Arlene knifed her dry tuna and Binnie scraped a forkful of beans. Then Albert stuck his pinkie stub against his nose, a decades-old nose-picking joke. Binnie sputtered a half-laugh.

"Gross, Dad."

"Oh, Al."

"Well, it works, doesn't it?"

Arlene brought out the baked yams for dessert.

"Want to make 'em tropical?"

They sprinkled the yams with coconut rum, a tiny bottle they'd acquired on their vacation in Puerto Rico a year ago. They weren't really rum drinkers, except when it came to fruity dessert. God, thought Binnie, that teeny tiny bottle.

"Speaking of work," Binnie said, raking her fork through glops of rummy yam, somewhat enjoying an upwelling of spite. "I'm thinking of moving to the city. That commute can be tiresome on a late night."

"Give up Aunt Ruby's apartment?"

"Well," said Binnie, chest tightening, "yeah."

"Oh, honey," said Arlene, her eyes going glassy. "I don't think that's a good idea." Binnie sucked her cheeks. A bubble of burnt yam sugar sat toward the rim of her plate. She'd taken the charred stuff of her own volition; she'd pictured it in the oven, syrup bursting through the skin. It was good, until it wasn't. "Think of all the money you're saving. You're set for life." Her father's nose whistled, a few bristly hairs poking out the nostrils.

Binnie tapped at the char. It crumbled, easily. Crème brûlée, à la Chez Greenson. Her mouth curled. "It just doesn't feel safe and all, when I'm on the subway all alone at nine o'clock." She hoped they wouldn't ask about the black cars she could take when she worked that late, the fancy cars that whisked her home any time she worked past eight. Living in Manhattan would be liberating. The idea of adulthood she'd had as a child.

"Well, it seems like an enormous waste to me."

Al patted Arlene's arm.

Binnie mashed her finger into the charcoal. Of course she'd been grateful for Ruby's apartment. She'd been grateful and grateful and grateful. Charred crumbs stuck to her skin. But at what cost? It was a never-ending cycle. Don't want a bat mitzvah? Do it for Ruby and you'll reap the rewards. Want to go to college? Study something "useful" or foot the bill. Whatever support was lovingly offered came with strings, and she was starting to feel beholden. Stifled. And here she was acting like a child, pouting over her dessert and justifying her choices to her parents. Why?

Binnie carried the dessert plates into the kitchen. Arlene said, "Thank you, honey," satisfied that she'd gotten the last word. There was no arguing with her. Hot water blasted the dishes. Let her think what she'll think.

Meanwhile, Binnie would think her own thoughts and go her own way. Stop living in Ruby's tomb.

Maybe a new place would grant her a sense of artistic freedom, she thought, as she scrubbed. Shake things up. And she could sleep later, be home quicker. Not marinate in the scent of ancient mothballs. Whatever she found would be considerably smaller and more expensive, but then wouldn't that be the true New York City experience? As a small girl she'd assumed that by twenty-five she'd be married and living in one of those castle-like buildings next to Central Park, a great big sparkler on her manicured ring finger. A babysitter had patted her curly head as a toddler, saying, "Oh you'll be a looker—marry rich, kid." No dice. *Ha*.

She left her parents to brew their after-dinner chamomile tea and peered into her old bedroom, now what her parents referred to as the den. Her father's stack of spy thrillers and Star Trek novels had doubled in size, wobbling toward the height of their matching ochre velour armchairs. Her mother's books, neatly stacked on a shelf, remained the same: Mitch Albom's entire oeuvre, a dozen historical romances arranged by era, and the well-thumbed pea-green tome titled *Heal Yourself Today*. Dozens of Starship Enterprise models cluttered the remaining shelves. Yarn and crochet needles lay on a side table in a snarl. All evidence of Binnie's life in that room gone.

"Want to stay for *Mystery*?" asked Arlene from the hall. "It's probably a rerun, but your father never remembers."

"No thanks. I don't want to get used to television again."

"All right, dear. We loved seeing you. Let's not let weeks go by like that again."

Binnie exhaled as she descended the cabbage-scented, faux-granite stairway. She rather liked her new idea of moving to the city. She'd said it out of spite, and now she simply had no choice but to follow through. She had to show her mother she could go it alone. That she could, in fact, be fully independent. She could never say: it's Ruby's tomb. Yes, it was huge with charming archways between the foyer and living room and creaky wood floors and a built-in glass-door spice cabinet in the kitchen that had stirred little Binnie's imagination—yes—but it was also dark and overheated in winter and dank in summer and tainted by sad personal history. She could never say: Ruby died alone, scared, unfulfilled, her brightest days a rosy memory of suitors shiny with Brilliantine cream. She could never say: this is part of some great long string of disappointment. Following the expected steps of your generation. Bitterly, she smiled.

It was time to cut the cord.

Before she hardened into a stone baby.

❖ ❖ ❖

On the way to the Fort Hamilton Parkway station, Binnie passed a young couple in elfin hipster shoes. The man's were lime green with trapezoidal toes and the woman's burnt orange and curved at the tip. They glanced at her, then glanced away, almost ashamed, as if coming home to Kensington was not nearly as cool as coming home to Williamsburg, which was what their outfits aspired to. Binnie recalled exploring Williamsburg as a high schooler, with a *Time Out New York* map in hand, and remarking that it seemed like a strange artsy college town that had been airlifted into northern Brooklyn. Eight years later it was a different thing again, gone on to the next stage of development, with pricey boutiques and high-end restaurants and narrow sidewalks crammed with shoppers and SUV-sized baby strollers. Park Slope had long been through this, but no one ever thought of non-brownstone Brooklyn, no one thought of the vast swath south of Prospect Park. In a way, Binnie too felt shame, and at the same time pride. This is real, authentic Brooklyn, not those northern parts with the gentrifying interlopers.

But was she somehow one of the interlopers, even as a born-and-bred Brooklynite? Was she a traitor, wanting to move to Manhattan and pretending she was one of the conquering hordes? Shouldn't she feel a little pride in the slow trickle of artsy types, even if they only showed their faces late in the night, for fear of recognizing each other in a not-cool part of Brooklyn? Wasn't *she* an artsy type? Hadn't she hated that friend of Ellen's who had moved to New York and refused to consider living anywhere but Manhattan even though it meant her rent would eat more than half her income and she'd still be in a rat hole? She'd hated that stupid bitch. And here she was, wanting the same.

Sliding into a bright orange seat on the F train, she unclenched her fists. She expelled a long, yogic breath, the kind of breath Beatrice used in the face of chaos. There is no need to feel angry. No need. The train shot out toward the Fourth Avenue station over the glittering Gowanus Canal. The blue Lowe's sign glowed in the night, reflecting on the black water. She stepped off to transfer, nearly slipping on a piece of detritus on the platform. A photograph. She kept her toe on it so that the wind would not blow it away as the train exited the station, whip it up and over, into the tracks. Bent down to pick it up. A little boy, age five or so, with a paper party hat, sitting at a bright yellow fast food restaurant table and happily eating soft-serve vanilla ice cream, a gleam of sweet cream on his smile. He wore a plaid, long-sleeved shirt, a relic of the early '80s. Who'd lose a photo like this, just leave it flapping in the wind? The platform was empty. She pocketed the artifact, feeling lucky.

At home, with her coat and shoes still on and the steam heat clanking, Binnie switched on the incandescent light above her work table and emptied a box of stale fruit candy, sorting out the yellow ones. The boy would be a character in a new diorama, and the yellow jujubes would be its center of gravity. She would shellac them together and they'd lend the thing, whatever it was, an unearthly translucence. She would make a wooden box for it. Maybe she would paint the box and bake it the way Cornell baked his painted boxes to weather them. Instant antiques. She stalked into the kitchen and nabbed a dusty container of turmeric, grabbed a circular from the recycling bin and sprinkled on it a ring of the marigold-colored powder. Marigolds. Would those fit? They would add whimsy, perhaps. Silk marigolds.

The window shuddered in its wood frame as she thrust it upward. She glued the little candies together with fast-acting glue, careful not to let it ooze, then shook her can of shellac, shielded her nose and mouth with one arm, and sprayed for a good hard minute. Then she rested, feeling giddy. The jujubes clustered together like something she'd seen in a science magazine. A magnified organism. A viral infection.

# Chapter Two

SUNLIGHT WARMED Binnie's pale, thin forearm. A metal keypad surgically implanted there, she imagined sleepily, could thwart reveries with electric zaps. The zaps would travel up her arm, which arranged and rearranged disparate objects into dream boxes—flotsam à la Joseph Cornell: cheap toys, hard candy, vintage cut-outs, things grasping at wonder—and, by entering her brain, kill the desire to make art. One could devise a quasi-Victorian design for such a contraption, wires entwining with nerves, all the way up to the frontal lobe. *Zip.* There goes your inner life. *Zap.* Back to work.

She descended into the subway with *Utopia Parkway*, a biography of Cornell that she read intermittently, hoping it would help her find her own path. He, too, had an overbearing mother. His day jobs gave him headaches and stomachaches, just like Binnie's. His diary entries chronicled airy lunches: red jam rolls, lemon cake, chocolate egg creams. Aunt Ruby could have been one of the girls lunching in automats that Cornell brooded over. Prim and oblivious to him. When she used to lean in to kiss Binnie as a girl she'd smelled of rose perfume and cold cream.

The first time Aunt Ruby ever opted not to pinch her cheek was after her bat mitzvah. Binnie hadn't wanted a bat mitzvah. She hated the idea of standing before her peers on the bimah, her dress from Sears scrutinized and, later, her temple basement party so sad compared to others' splashy affairs: custom t-shirts torpedoed out of a canon! a Noah's Ark–themed cruise around Manhattan! An Absolut Vodka ad–themed shindig at the Brooklyn Botanic Garden! Arlene had been appalled at the latter. A bad girl boast. In any case, Arlene begged Binnie to have a bat mitzvah for Aunt Ruby's sake, Binnie being the closest thing to a granddaughter she would ever have. So she did. Aunt Ruby, dark bobbed hair perfectly sleek, expertly lined eyes watering, kvelled and kvelled.

As she marched up the grimy steps from the subway platform, a little ball of hate the size of a marble stuck in her throat, the sort of quiet hate a child feels for a place they do not wish to go, but must. To work. To battle for money, not hers.

The bustle of midtown on a Monday morning was in stark contrast to the prior two weeks. The darkened windows of downtown Wilmington's old stone buildings had summoned Cornell's haunted palace in "Setting for a Fairy Tale": a crowd of thin white trees rising up behind its gabled roof, stark against an inky black sky. In Wilmington the spookiness was real, boarded-up retail and "For Lease" signs dismal. Panhandlers grimmer than New York's homeless. With so few people on the street, who would seek charity in such a city?

The marble of hate slunk to Binnie's stomach. She envisioned a diorama in the shape of a Beaux Arts bank, its roof caving in. The diorama would sit on a low pedestal, so that you could look down the hole in its top, and a mirror inside, angled just so, would make the darkness infinite. Title: "Black Hole".

"Welcome back," Madeline said in her subtle, lilting British-Caribbean accent. Her high cheekbones framed a curious smile. Did Binnie look disheveled? Pissed to be back? Two weeks of trial in Wilmington and nothing but a weekend to wash away the bad taste of losing.

The Zombie's terrible smoker's cough, a long and tortured rattling of phlegm, resounded through the closed door of the firm's one windowless office. A set of venetian blinds covered the window on the door, shutting out the Zombie's one chance for diffuse natural light, but they could not hide the odor of cigarettes. *Richard Jones*, his nameplate said. Everyone but Madeline called him Dick, and maybe it was immature of Binnie to think this was a private joke in the office, yet he never seemed to insist on being called Richard or even Jones. Madeline used "Mr." with the partners but not anyone else. He was Richard to her alone and it sounded grand in her accent. Madeline picked up the phone, dispelling any need for Binnie to attempt small talk. Into the center of the Lipstick's ellipse she went (the building was not round but oval), to her kitchen-adjacent cubicle.

❖ ❖ ❖

Down the hall, a woman knelt outside Capra's door, shining his shoes while he ate an apple and read the paper. A regular ritual. Following the firm's hierarchy, Zaiman would be next, then Baxter. Apparently embarrassed by the image of a woman kneeling before them to shine their shoes, they all opted to slip off their oxfords each morning and let her shine them in the hallway. Binnie preferred the lawyers unshod.

In the kitchen, with supreme care, she refilled the faux-ebony box of espresso pods. *Robust, earthy, fruity, floral, light*—the tasting notes of purple, gold, black, green, and copper pods arranged in tidy lines. Little caffeine soldiers in colorful helmets. The pods had Italian names: Arpeggio, Lungo, Maestro.

What about an assemblage like that. Like "Taglioni's Jewel Casket," a velvet-lined box Joseph Cornell had made in homage to the Romantic-era ballerina Marie Taglioni, who travelled with a "jewel casket" full of precious stones gifted to her by European royalty. Instead of gems, Cornell filled the box with neat rows of glass ice cubes from a dime store and strung fake diamonds along the top. The word casket, of course, elicited the notion of death. Like the box was some relic buried in a sumptuous tomb. The name "Coffee Casket" exuded much less magic. "Capra's Coffee Casket"? No, no, no. Maybe instead of espresso pods she'd use gum drops. And a candy necklace? "Gum Drop Casket"—now that title sparkled.

A postcard of Cornell's "Untitled (Marine Fantasy with Tamara Toumanova)" hung beside her computer. In a striped purple-red bodice vaguely resembling veins and an expansive skirt of kelp and fleshy seaweed, the ballerina floated with hands and face poised upward in calm exultation. Silver, red-gold, and green-dappled fish swam; murky butterflies flew; coral grasped and sea vegetables swayed.

*Sleep with the fishes*, she thought, of Peter Pan's Casinos. Wasn't all of the "gaming industry" the mob anyway? She was surprised when neither side displayed the stereotypical appearance of mafiosos. Nary a pinkie ring in the bunch.

Baxter skulked toward Binnie's desk. Without his suit coat he appeared stringy. His salt-and-pepper hair flopped a bit as he skulked.

"Hey, Binnie," he muttered. In Delaware she had pitied it, that voice thickened by the loss of the trial, but now? He swiveled, his anxious body always fidgeting, drummed at the wall of her cubicle. Wouldn't meet her eye. "We've gotta get started on this appeal. Rick'll help, right Rick?"

Zaiman, in his office across from Binnie's cubicle, rustled *The Wall Street Journal* and said, "Work on the appeal? Maybe they could pay some bills first?" Through the open door Binnie could see his view of the East River.

Baxter's face darkened into the guise of a fox, the wily fox Rick had long ago warned Binnie about, the one wracked by indecision and which had no qualms about keeping them in the office late into the night, dismantling briefs he changed his mind about, re-copying and re-assembling them. Baxter did not turn to acknowledge Zaiman. Rick poked his head up from his cubicle, which shared a half-wall with Binnie's on one side and Beatrice's on the other. "Hm?"

"PanCorp!" said Baxter.

"Yes. PanCorp."

"All right," said Baxter. "Go team." He slapped the top of the cubicle wall once more before loping away.

"Do you really need my help?" Rick asked. "I'm very busy with OilCo." His shoulder, in a crisp pink shirt, gave a little twitch of pride. PanCorp was the case for losers; OilCo was the real-deal big money promising a juicy bonus at the end of it.

"Well," said Binnie, "I don't really know what I'm doing, so...a little help would be nice. Five minutes of guidance?"

Rick huffed and led the way toward the windowless file room at the center of the office. The air of disregard he seemed to carry about him, the feeling that at any minute he might casually say or do something cruel, brought to mind a red-kneed little boy calmly burning ants with magnifying glasses.

Aside from PanCorp and OilCo, business slowed that week. On Friday, Beatrice and Capra joked wistfully in the kitchen that despite the economic downturn, it wouldn't be long before people would be litigating again. It was good to be in bankruptcy.

At 4:00 p.m. Zaiman said, "I'm outta here. Going to catch *Double Indemnity* at Lincoln Center."

"Barbara Stanwyck," Capra said. "What a broad."

Zaiman said, "Why doesn't everyone scram?"

Binnie slurped cold, sour coffee and felt the glee and dread of being cut loose early on a Friday, freedom by way of drying-up prospects. Pulling on a wool coat riddled with pilled lint, she remembered her little boy with the vanilla ice cream mouth and told herself the high-wire act to come was absolutely necessary to her progress.

On First Avenue, not too far from 53rd, an antique shop displayed an "apartment for rent" sign in the window. The shop's hours were "by chance or by appointment," the handwritten sign water-stained and curling, the brown paint at the doorway thick and flaking. There was no phone number on the rent sign. A chill crept into the air, cutting through the gold-tinted autumn light. Binnie peered through the dirty window and knocked. An old woman in a quilted housecoat opened the door halfway.

"Yes?"

"I'd like to see the apartment for rent."

The woman shut the door. Binnie stood around, unsure how long to wait. The woman came back in a wool pea coat. Her white hair, soft and curly, had a touch of blond in it. She had a dour face and steely eyes and a long gray hair on her chin.

She jangled a big chain of keys. "This way *please*." They walked up a narrow, creaking staircase that leaned slightly to the right. At the landing were two doors. The woman opened one of them.

"It's an efficiency," she said. "Or a studio, whatever you call 'em these days."

The linoleum in the seafoam-green kitchenette was dirty and cracked, the wood floors of the living area rough and scratched. Splotches mottled the only two windows, which faced First Avenue. A brown refrigerator gurgled. Sticky mouse traps clustered behind the front door, flecked with the carcasses of fruit flies.

Binnie stuck her head in the tiny, pink-tiled bathroom and flushed the toilet, which was thankfully turdless (she'd suspected she'd find one just waiting for her in there). She turned on the sink and the shower and the gas stove and saw that everything worked okay. The colors were kind of nauseating but at the same time the combination worked. There was a history here, but it wasn't her history. Or that of anyone she knew. She could make the space her own.

"How much?"

"For you?"

"Uh, yeah, for me."

The woman appraised Binnie's outfit; her darting eyes calculated demeanor. "$1300. Plus first, last, and security."

This was double the price for less than half the space Binnie had in Aunt Ruby's place. Plus questionable atmosphere, though the woman and her store might add a saltiness to Binnie's life that she could learn to appreciate. Actually, the price seemed kind of low, given the area.

"I should add I'm your upstairs neighbor *and* your downstairs neighbor, and the gentleman across the hall from you is my estranged husband." She crossed her arms. "We've owned this building for thirty years."

"I work long hours. You'll barely see me."

"Deal."

Outside, the cold air perked Binnie up. She was happy to have the place, happy to have the process be quick, not some stressful, drawn-out affair. The gold-tinted light shifted to twilit indigo.

Binnie ended her other lease.

"You could've sublet the place, Binnie," Arlene shouted on the phone. Binnie imagined the blue vein pulsing in her mother's temple. "Your timing is spectacularly bad."

Binnie put on a cool, collected voice. "Oh well, Ma. You live, you learn."

The following Friday night, she used an entire bottle of Soft Scrub and two rolls of paper towels scouring the place as hard as she could. She made a greasy mess of the wood floors, finding comfort in the smells of bleach and Murphy's Oil Soap. *Drill baby drill*, Sarah Palin had said at the Vice Presidential debate the night before. Binnie hadn't watched—she didn't have a TV—but Zaiman had relished the ridiculousness in the office all day. "I can see Russia from my house!" he added, channeling Tina Fey's impersonation in a ditzy falsetto. Laugh all you want, Rick had muttered. Laugh all the way to the bank.

*Let me smudge your new place*, Ellen texted.

*That sounds dirty.*

*You'll thank me later!*

Ellen showed up despite Binnie's protests. A bundle of sage in one hand, a box of matches in the other. She lit the herbs on fire and wafted smoke into all the studio's crevices. Binnie worried that all the chemical fumes combining would cause an explosion.

"I'm airing out the nasty," Ellen said.

"If you say so. Help me move tomorrow?"

"Sorry. I have plans."

She planted a big kiss on Binnie's cheek on her way out. "Text me in the afternoon. I'll try to find time."

The next day Gary helped Binnie with multiple trips on the subway. She piled garbage bags into a granny cart. He lugged boxes on a hand cart.

"There's gotta be a better way," Binnie said, already tired after the first leg of their journey.

"Like, hire other people to do this? With a van and stuff? That would be brilliant." They laughed.

After each descent to the platform, they collapsed on the shiny hard seats with a sigh and a smile. Each ascent of the enormous escalator at the Lexington Avenue stop offered another welcome moment of repose. Even if they were in a subterranean tunnel. Even if subway stalactites mysteriously dripped.

On their second trip a gaggle of preschool-aged children—hopped up, no doubt, on Saturday morning cartoons and Fruit Loops—swarmed around them, clambering on the seats on either side. Maybe headed to Central Park, to the playground near the Met's Temple of Dendur. The structure of that playground—tunneled mounds, perfect for humans under four feet—and the experience of being inside an ancient temple, transported from Egypt and reconstructed in a gallery filled with air and light, had long been implanted in Binnie's consciousness. She'd been to the Dendur many times and lamented, as she grew, being unable to fit inside the playground's best structures. But the stone of the temple, salvaged before the Nile flooded, held a certain power. Something of the past not entirely lost.

However purloined.

"Gingerbread Temple": Pudgy-kneed children made of almond paste swarm a graham cracker Dendur, scaling its ridges, nibbling its columns and cornices, lapping at a reflecting pool of blue-dyed vanilla frosting. A candied hippopotamus peeps out of the water, snout flared, anticipating the snap of their fat little thighs. She would have to shellac it to make it last, but that would take the fun out of working with food. Candy too old to eat was a better material.

The children were now quacking like ducks. Their father/uncle/nanny loomed over them, trying to stop them from squirming off the seats and losing their balance with the train's sway. From clunking into a metal pole and crying. Gary scrunched his face and smiled, eyes shining with a level of aliveness she'd yet to see in him. She suppressed the urge to run her fingertip along his long brown lashes. His eyes unscrunched, as if he sensed her urge. Her body hummed with hope and happiness.

Binnie didn't own much furniture. Ruby's floral brocade sofa, which would not fit in her new studio, was destined for the building's basement laundry room, a perch for little old ladies who found the journey between loads cumbersome. She pictured them settling into the sagging cushions, paging through murder mysteries and bodice-rippers while waiting for a dryer to become available. Arlene would hate to hear about this, but Binnie didn't want to discuss the move with her anymore, even though in truth it felt a little like a betrayal. The last relic of Ruby abandoned in a basement laundry room.

Her work table they dismantled and were able to transport by subway on the third trip, when Ellen actually lent a hand—Binnie hid her assemblage materials in a sealed cardboard box inside a sealed garbage bag before her friends arrived. Aunt Ruby's cut-glass perfume bottle nested at the center of her materials, wrapped in a layer of tissue paper, a layer of newspaper, bubble wrap, and packing tape. The one thing from Ruby's place she truly needed. Not the pre-war apartment. Just the perfume bottle. The revelation of this difference, perfume bottle not apartment, buoyed her upward. She felt lighter, freer. Agile. Through all its protective wrappings, the cut-glass bottle glowed. Portability!

The bed was a problem.

"Burn it," said Ellen.

"Ellen!" said Binnie.

"What? It's not like you can sell that thing."

Binnie nodded. It was a terrible bed. She could barely remember how she'd acquired it, from a roommate of a friend of a friend, but she hadn't paid a cent for it. Arlene had consented to donate Ruby's simple oak-frame to Goodwill before Binnie moved in and had the mattress hauled away to the dump. Ruby had died in that bed. Arlene at least understood that.

"There's a thing called Freecycle," said Gary. "You could give it away and someone will take it off your hands for free." They posted onto Freecyle and Craigslist and sat on the floor in Aunt Ruby's place playing cards until someone called.

"It have bedbugs?" asked the woman.

"No, never," said Binnie.

"Hang on, my husband'll get it."

They dismantled the bed. A man with scars all over his arms came and said he could get the bed home in two cab rides. They helped him lash the mattress to the car's roof and as it pulled away, Binnie asked, "Knife fight, you think?" One August, when Binnie was changing buses in Albany, a topless man had sauntered around the station, his back splotched with bullet wound scars, shiny and thick.

"Well, he's not a cutter," Gary said.

Ellen's eyes flickered at Gary. "No."

Half an hour later they helped the man lash the metal frames atop the taxi. The cabbie frowned but complied. The car started moving before the man even closed the passenger door.

"What do I sleep on now?" Binnie asked.

"You're nearly a grownup in a studio of your very own," said Ellen. "Go get yourself a nice futon."

Binnie sighed. They went to a cheap furniture store near NYU and paid the extra $50 for delivery and by 8:00 p.m. she had a studio full of boxes and garbage bags and a place to sleep that wasn't the floor.

"Boxes depress me," said Ellen. "Let's go out for dinner."

Over massaman curry and garlic naan, Ellen told Gary and Binnie about how she was going to Amsterdam over Thanksgiving weekend for a quick get-away and to see Damien Hirst's "For the Love of God," a diamond-encrusted skull with real human teeth. Her eyes glittered as she spoke of the many diamonds and the many carats and what a splash the auction had been when it sold last year to a private investment firm for a hundred million. Gary and Binnie quietly "mmhmmed." Gary made eyes at Binnie, who slid her eyes sideways, feeling fuzzy inside. He looked like he might reach across the table to grab her hands if it wasn't for Ellen. Warm orange-red chili-shaped lights and multicolored Christmas lights lit up the walls of the restaurant.

Smiling into her Kingfisher beer, she felt as if a whole egg were in her belly and it had ever so slightly cracked.

"So. Are you coming to the holiday party?"

The warm yolky feeling in Binnie's belly quickly congealed. "Oh—I guess? It's so far off still."

"Actually, it isn't. And you should bring a little something to show Alexis."

"Is that how it works?" She guzzled her beer, feeling hopeful but apprehensive. Just show up at the gallery with a "little something"? It seemed foolhardy.

Gary asked, "Can I come?"

Ellen broke into a grin. "You can be Binnie's date."

"I've always wanted to be arm candy."

"Well," said Ellen, "that settles it. You have some work to do, Binnie."

She did have work to do. She resented the push but knew it to be true. Ellen and Gary escorted Binnie back toward her new little nest, Ellen in the middle linking arms with both of them. Taxis zoomed by in yellow flashes. The occasional horn in the distance, reverberating against the urban canyons, thrilled Binnie. Was it dumb to be excited about living in Manhattan? Six legs crossed the street in lockstep and she thought *this is my life now* and smiled, felt the wind on her teeth.

"It's so nice out," Binnie said. She didn't want the night to end. "Why don't we go down to the river?" They steered east, to a little wooded park by the FDR.

"Nice," said Ellen. "Nice, nice, nice."

A tiny slice of the city she'd yet to experience? A new, unconsidered vista? Gold star for Binnie: Ellen's approval was rare. It was like finally grabbing the brass ring, and Binnie hated herself, just a little bit, for this feeling, this enjoyment of her approval. But she felt it. In their friendship Binnie was constantly offering herself up to Ellen, asking, *Am I any good?*

The scent of the Atlantic, cold and briny, laced the breeze.

"How many people swim across that river?" Gary wondered. In the dark, Binnie could decipher the outlines of the ruin on Roosevelt Island, the old insane asylum exposed by the muckraker Nelly Bly—she'd written a report on her in the sixth grade, still remembered it. A unit called "Great New Yorkers."

"I bet a swim through that really brings out your third eye," said Ellen. Before anyone could respond she said, "Okay, your most common anxiety dream. Go."

"The one where you forget to go to school for a year," said Gary. "Yet show up to the final exam knowing you know nothing and that you should have known something by now. Every damn time."

"Mine's the naked one," said Ellen. "Standing on a street corner in a top but no pants."

Feeling smug, relishing having the best one, Binnie said, "Eating glass."

"*Glass*, Binnie?" Ellen tugged at her arm.

"Sure. Glass."

"What's wrong with you?"

"Second most common: swallowing my own teeth. You don't get those dreams? What about choking on a giant wad of bubble gum? Or the one with the enormous whack-a-moles?"

"No, I only have the naked ones."

Gary said, "I'd like to spend an hour in your brain, Binnie."

"More like in her pants," Ellen snorted.

"It's a real circus in there," said Binnie, ignoring Ellen, training her eyes on Gary, still buzzed from the beer. "An army of mechanical monkeys banging on drums."

Someone shuffled toward them. A homeless man with a hospital bracelet around his bony wrist and gray bandages around his forearms, asking for change. A string of saliva hung from his bottom lip, which drooped away from his face.

"Sorry!" said Ellen. She pulled Gary and Binnie away.

The man grunted and ambled past them, toward the edge of the park.

Gary said, "He's in rough shape."

"Yeah," Binnie said. A strange thing to see in this tonier part of town. The rawness was getting so saturated it leached through previous barriers. A crack in a dam. Kensington wasn't as grim, though she'd spied an elderly neighbor of her parents stooping with difficulty toward a discarded melon in a grocer's trash heap once.

Ellen's brows knit for a fleeting moment. "The vulnerable will be affected first and worst."

Binnie shook her head at the exchange of Things Compassionate Adults Say and glanced over her shoulder at the man, who was now urinating in an arc over the sidewalk, his head craned up to the sky and his mouth wide open. She could still see the string of saliva gleaming under the street lamp.

On Sunday morning, she haphazardly unpacked. She thought of the potential of the "Infection" diorama, the incoherence of her other materials. She wanted "Infection" to spread to new pieces, to replicate, mutate. She wanted to ask Ellen for advice: how did all those people at her gallery make their start? But she was afraid of the possible answers and how they might relate to her—connections (a possibility, thanks to Ellen), inherited wealth (nope), abject poverty (a possibility), immense sacrifice (maybe?).

Talent.

Luck.

# Chapter Three

BEATRICE LIMPED AROUND the office after a morning with the sadistic personal trainer who had her on a regimen of hundreds of daily squats. Sipping a jumbo green smoothie, she gave Binnie a print-out of a cleanse diet Gwyneth Paltrow had recommended; Binnie put it in her purse to throw out later. Binnie knew Beatrice wasn't Jewish, but something about this performance suggested atonement.

"Sugar is death," Beatrice said grimly. Then moaned, "I would *kill* for a potato chip."

"We need to talk about the bills," Capra said, halfway across the room. Beatrice let out a yogic fire breath.

In faint pencil Binnie sketched how she imagined Ellen's boss Alexis: a patrician fifty-something woman with Susan Sontag hair, black with a shock of white. She'd never met her, never seen her, only met Ellen outside of the gallery for infrequent jaunts to expensive cocktail bars of Ellen's choosing. Once that summer, while Binnie loitered on the sidewalk waiting for Ellen to wrap up inside, a man had commented on her silver cherry blossom necklace.

"That's a traditional Japanese fertility symbol."

"Interesting," Binnie said.

"Not really," said the man, pleased with himself. Binnie had peered through the window at Ellen, willing her to cut her schmoozing short.

She couldn't afford to have that attitude anymore. She would go to the gallery holiday party. She would get Alexis's card. This was part of the deal with herself, the one where she gave up the yoke of Aunt Ruby's place and struck out on her own.

Two cubicles over, Beatrice and Capra soberly discussed which bills would not be paid. Binnie had never eavesdropped on such a conversation before and certainly not in the workplace. Belt tightening, sure. Bill skipping? She hadn't known that was an option. She just ate less and less, cheaper and cheaper. But there was a limit to that. Scurvy, for starters.

How extravagant life had seemed the night before the start of the trial. Debauched, even. Capra's mistress came down to join them in Wilmington and they were all supposed to accept it as easily as Binnie picking up Capra's dry cleaning for him. They went to dinner with the clients. Binnie met Zaiman, Capra, Baxter, and Georgina in the hotel lobby. Capra was off in a corner calling some cabs. Georgina jumped into Baxter's lap. Binnie tried not to stare but from the corner of her eye she stared. Binnie and Georgina were roughly the same age. Georgina had a skinny heroin-chic thing going on, a delicate face, sharp cheeks and chin, little pointed nose, dark hair, and dark, wide-set eyes; Binnie felt fat and pasty next to her. Though once that summer, Baxter had said Binnie didn't need to watch her weight, and as she walked away from him she felt his eyes on the A-line of her polka dot skirt.

"Hi!" Georgina chirped.

"Hi," said Baxter, with a strange smile. Not quite lascivious. Not quite uncomfortable. But in a Venn diagram of the two qualities, it was a dot just outside the overlap.

"Miss me?"

Zaiman and Baxter must have been used to Georgina's antics, since neither of them flinched. If anything, Baxter seemed embarrassed that Binnie was there. As if it would have been fine with just Georgina and the guys.

Zaiman turned away from Georgina, perched on Baxter's knee, and murmured something about the inevitable Capra Zaiman sexual harassment suit. He wasn't looking at Binnie when he said this, but she was sure it was directed at her. Like Binnie could sue for that: another woman on a partner's lap. When Capra got off the phone, Georgina scampered over to him and he hugged her from behind. It appeared terribly possessive, an obvious showing off of his half-his-age girlfriend.

Baxter was biting his cuticles.

"I guess that's better than smoking," Zaiman said, averting his gaze from the lovebirds.

"Gimme a break," said Baxter.

They piled into two cabs.

The cavernous restaurant was in a former warehouse. Blue lights backlit tall vases of smooth, spindly branches. The clients, two hedge fund managers who'd bought a majority stake in Peter Pan's Casinos in early 2001 and were now being sued by a group of its creditors, were already there. Ron Harrison of Neptune Management was a short, slight man with hang-dog eyes. Fred Olsen of Tychee Financial was sturdy and tall, and one of his blue eyes seemed darker. Duller. Didn't show a gleam of understanding: a glass eye. Binnie focused on his active eye, wondering what polite society dictated in such situations. What would Ruby do? *Don't stare.* Olsen nodded politely to Binnie when they shook hands and gave curt nods when other people spoke, only offering his opinion when expressly asked. Binnie moved away and stood near Harrison instead. She didn't know what to say. All she knew of him was that in the office Baxter avoided his persistent calls until Zaiman cracked the whip and told him to make a decision, move forward. They managed five minutes of idle chit-chat but his eyes kept their wounded look the whole time, suggesting a sense of profound injustice performed for Binnie to decipher.

At a round table, Georgina sat between Capra and Binnie. Olsen sat on Binnie's other side. Harrison, Baxter, and Zaiman rounded the circle back to Capra. Binnie felt nervous about the prospect of making conversation with Olsen, yet something about his general (Scandinavian?) reticence comforted her. Georgina ordered a Chopin vodka martini.

"I have Celiac's disease," she said to Binnie.

"Oh?"

"Chopin is the only vodka I can have."

"It's made from potatoes." An ad Binnie had seen for the drink came to mind. A woman with perfectly round breasts, wearing a tall fur cap, pouring the cold clear liquid. Binnie realized she'd just repeated the slogan out loud. *It's made from potatoes.*

"Right."

Binnie felt lame for ordering chardonnay, but she didn't want to get drunk, and red wine gave her headaches and stained her lips and teeth. Capra also had a martini. Zaiman had scotch; the rest ordered beer. Everyone but Binnie ordered spinach salad to start. Spinach was the leaf of the era, taking over romaine, which had in turn taken over iceberg. But Binnie didn't want to order the same thing as everyone else, and the only other salad was garden salad, a sad array of iceberg lettuce and stale shredded carrots. Oh well, she thought. White wine and iceberg. She felt herself disappearing into the wall. Except Georgina kept talking to her.

"So, that guy from SNL, Seth Meyers, he totally hit on me in a bar last night."

"Oh?"

"I was like, whatever."

The salad came and went. Binnie rounded out her series of bland choices with a grilled chicken breast and vegetable medley. Georgina ordered steak tartare and a second martini. Capra glared at her.

Georgina rolled her eyes. "He can't keep up," she muttered. "I drink with my clients all the time." The second martini lowered before her on a tray and her eyes said to the waitress: bless you. She leaned toward Binnie. Her speech increased in speed and lowered in volume. "Have you met Harrison before? He's so gross. He totally hit on me."

"Did he?" Binnie lowered her voice too. "That *is* gross."

"Yeah. It's sad. He's kind of a mealy pig. What college did you go to? I miss college. I was on the swim team and Model UN."

Binnie wondered if Georgina was younger than she'd previously thought. The loud music made it difficult for her to hear everything being said. She supposed she could say what she did in college for fun, but she hadn't been on any kind of sports team or part of any kind of club. She reshelved books in the library for four years, a task that became gloomier when Arlene stopped paying tuition and Binnie piled on student loans. She'd been too shy, also, to do the artsy activities she should have done, all-night art-making marathons in the student union, elaborate costumes for a drag ball. Her diligence at the library got her promoted to the special collections. There'd been some artist books there and she'd become enamored with dreamy, obscure objects, like a book in the shape of a bed, with embroidered quilts and pillow cases serving as pages. She wanted to make dreamy stuff like that, stuff of wonder. She couldn't begin to explain it.

The main course arrived, but Georgina only moved the food around on her plate.

"You know, I can barely eat a thing. I have colitis. Nothing agrees with me."

"I'm sorry."

Was she saying this to bond with Binnie? Was Binnie now supposed to divulge something personal to Georgina? Or was she just making something up to cover for an eating disorder?

"I went to a small school upstate," Binnie said.

"What?"

"You asked me what college I went to. I went upstate. You probably haven't heard of it. Near Colgate. But not Colgate."

"Oh. Colgate. Cool. I went to Columbia."

"Oh."

Binnie didn't correct her. Georgina talked faster and faster at a lower and lower volume. Binnie could barely understand her. Something about first meeting Capra at a craps table in Vegas.

"At Peter Pan's?" Binnie asked. Georgina glanced at Harrison, then tilted her head at Binnie.

"Caesar's." This was before she was laid off. He liked a high roller, he'd said. He bought her a mink coat. In the desert.

Baxter wanted dessert, but no one else did. He ordered a slice of flourless seven-layer chocolate ganache cake and eight spoons.

"C'mon," he said. "Everyone enjoy a bite."

Each diner took a teeny bite of the cake but still there was a healthy sliver left that no one would touch. Binnie felt bad about the waste but knew she couldn't be the person to finish the cake. It just seemed wrong. It would seem wrong for any of them, even if Baxter said

"atta boy" or "atta girl" to egg them on. Like the eater of
the leftovers was a chump. Gary would have swooped in
on it with good humor and relish. *Joke's on you*, he'd say,
dancing in his chair as he made the spoonful of mousse
last.

"I guess that's the sacrificial cake," Binnie said. Her
cheeks reddened as soon as the words came out of her
mouth. What a weird thing to say, she thought, sacrificial
cake, like she'd next toss a virgin on a pyre. Inexplicably,
Olsen let out a wild, hearty laugh. It was a strange
laugh, like he'd been overtaken by the sudden mania of
a Bacchanal. Perhaps he was overtired. Or perhaps they
were all doing coke behind her back.

He laughed and his head shook, and as he gasped
for air something plunked out of his face and cracked
against his chocolate-smeared plate. Shards of pale and
colored glass scattered onto the tablecloth, into Binnie
and Harrison's laps, and onto the floor.

"My eye!"

"Oh gosh," said Binnie. "I'm so sorry."

Everyone inspected the table, gathered the shards.
Binnie didn't want to see Olsen's gaping eye socket. She
crouched on the ground. Bits were on the black wood floor.
Striped black, blue, white. One inch-long crescent-shaped
chunk presented an inside texture like basalt. She slipped
the crescent chunk into her purse before gathering a few
tiny glass splinters into her palm as an offering.

"We'll replace it, Fred," Baxter said.

"Oh, you don't have to do that," Olsen said.

"I'm sorry," Binnie said again.

"It's not your fault," Olsen said. "It's all right."

"Do you have a spare in the meantime?" asked Capra, gently.

No one asked explicitly if he'd have to wear an eye patch on the witness stand, but that seemed to be the collective worry. A pirate banker would not do.

"I have my old one. This was just custom ordered from Switzerland. The glass had a special liveliness to it. I should've gotten used to it before wearing it out." Of course he wanted a nice eye for his day in court.

"You think they could put it back together?" said Baxter. "Let us know if we can help."

Olsen said he'd just have to get a new eye. The group grew somber. Binnie's purse hid the stolen eye shard, a secret that glowed and pulsated.

Back at the hotel, Georgina slipped her arm around Binnie's shoulder, like they were old pals. Her bony hip swayed against Binnie's, more than pal-ish. The partners trailed behind. Baxter and Zaiman's rooms were to the left of the elevators; Binnie, Capra, and Georgina's to the right.

"Have a good schluff," Baxter said as they parted ways.

Binnie wondered when Georgina would remove her arm, what she intended by lingering in front of Binnie's door.

"Well, good night," Binnie said.

"Good night," Capra said, beckoning Georgina down the hall. There it was, Binnie posited. Flirting with another woman to turn on a man. Georgina's motor-mouthing faded down the hall: *remember Tink's Table, remember Tink's tiny titties*? Capra uttered something sober-sounding before shutting their door.

Binnie stored the eye shard in a plastic film canister among her art materials. She thought and thought and thought about what do with it, but nothing came to her except Buñuel's *Un chien andalou*: clouds sliding across the moon, a knife slicing an eye. Not useful. She wasn't about to purchase sheep's eyes for the sake of art.

Rick sipped his eleven o'clock cup of tomato soup. He always had tomato soup for lunch at eleven and snacked on carrot sticks at three in the afternoon—he ate so many carrots he would turn orange. She wondered if all the acid from the tomatoes contributed to his unpleasant demeanor.

Baxter loafed by on his way to the coffee machine. "Beatrice, when you get a chance—that extra policy rider?"

"You get the doctor's report?" Her voice soft.

"Clean as a whistle."

"All right," Capra said.

Beatrice's thanks as Baxter left sounded strangely heavy.

Maybe, thought Binnie, she should take a sick day to prepare for her meeting with Alexis. (Meeting! As if Alexis knew she existed.) She made a list of what she would need for "Gingerbread Temple," which was almost everything. It felt dangerous, playing hooky. She got a grand total of five vacation days per year, plus two floating religious holidays. But sick days were unlimited, on an honor system—a blessing from a health scare Capra had suffered before Binnie's time at CZB. If he hadn't almost died, she assumed, they'd have a miserly allotment for illness too. He was still careful. The provision in his lunch chart for this week (the chart: a Byzantine spreadsheet designed by a nutrition-lifestyle guru and taped to Binnie's cubicle wall for her to manage) had been boiled parsnip, lightly massaged Tuscan kale salad, and a bottle of unsweetened cranberry juice, cut with Austrian mineral water hand-bottled in the Alps, by, Binnie couldn't help but suppose, angelic castrati in lederhosen.

Weeks passed with nary a sick day claimed. Binnie was being good, she told herself. Lunch at her desk, "forgotten" lunches, these were virtues in the workplace. She knew it was stupid, but things ran smoothly, and *smoothly* meant no one yelled, no one grumbled, no one cast glares of resentment her way. Time slipped past.

Giddiness over Election Day mounted. Ellen invited Binnie and Gary uptown to watch the pre–Election Day episode of *Saturday Night Live*. On her Space Age vermillion couch, a tubular L-shaped affair with rounded corners, Ellen opened a bottle of Cabernet Franc, popped the cork to everyone's glee. "I'm going to Bali in the spring," Ellen said, pouring wine into three monster goblets.

"Bally's?" asked Binnie.

"Bahli, Bahli. *Indonesia*. With Todd. Work's been stressful. Time for a getaway."

Oh yes. So stressful to anticipate spending Thanksgiving in Amsterdam gawping at diamonds-in-a-skull.

Binnie vowed to be excited for her friend. "First big trip. Getting serious?"

Ellen's face twisted, like Binnie had said the wrong thing. "Here, have some hard salami. Everyone needs a good hard salami, *amiright*?"

Binnie chewed on a round of meat.

"Is salami halal?" Gary asked, drily.

Ellen giggled, but it wasn't the braying guffaw that Binnie had come to identify as her genuine expression of pleasure. "Wrong island. Anyway, Todd's one hundred percent beef."

"They have a water religion," Binnie said, of Bali, but then the show came on and Ellen was already turning up the volume. There was a skit of the Obamas doing a variety show. Maya Rudolph as Michelle sang "Solid as Barack" and everyone smiled and smiled. Binnie felt a gleam of hope that everything might just work out.

During a commercial break, Ellen muted the television and leaned over Gary toward Binnie, shiny with anticipation. Binnie expected her to announce her latest epiphany in therapy: perhaps an irrational fear of Botero's nudes.

"How are your projects coming along?"

Ellen's rosy cheeks glowed. Binnie's splotched and flushed.

The blue light of the television flickered over Ellen's face, danced with the twinkle in her eye. She seemed to be calculating, waiting for Binnie to finally prove herself, finally show some goddamn confidence. *I have just the thing for Alexis*, she should say. *It will win her heart. It will blow her mind. In two years, I'll have a Guggenheim. In five years I'll be a MacArthur genius.*

Binnie's eyes darted around the apartment. Ellen shared a "one-bedroom-plus den" with Cass, an editorial intern at *Art Forum*. Ellen got the bedroom; feline Cass curled up in the nook that was the den, behind an Art Deco room divider.

In a pocket of quiet, Binnie detected the subtle sound of a page turning behind the room divider. Visualizing white earbuds plugged into Cass's elfin ears, she swirled the garnet wine.

"Oh, you know. Projects are good. Projects are coming along..."

Ellen drained her glass and said, with half a grin, "Well, y'know what they say. Either shit or get off the pot."

She snorted a short laugh. Gary's brown eyes softened into a sympathetic pudding. Ellen was sweeter when sober.

Binnie thought of biting through her goblet. It was delicate at the rim and sturdy at the base so that she could grasp it in her palm and shatter the top in her mouth easily enough. She set it down. The liquid gently sloshed.

Maya Rudolph couldn't reappear fast enough. Gary grabbed the remote and turned the sound on. It seemed the pudding of his eyes hardened; Binnie liked to think he was mad at Ellen. *Gary! Let the pudding skins fall from your eyes! I'm not worth the anger.* They settled back into Ellen's couch, a "reasonably priced" $3000 Roche Bobois.

Gary walked Binnie home. It was late, almost "anything-goes time," as Gary liked to call the weird hours between three and six in the morning; apparently it hadn't occurred to him that they could still take a cab, and the cross-town subway transfers would be annoying. Anyway, Binnie wanted to take a long walk with Gary. And it seemed he wanted to take a long walk with her.

"What was that?" Gary asked, a few steps out of Ellen's building. They thrust their hands in their pockets against the cold, sunk chins into coat collars.

"You mean with Ellen? Shit or get off the pot?"

"Yeah. It was kinda...harsh."

"I know. She's trying to push me, I guess. Y'know? Tough love."

A bus barreled down the otherwise empty street before he said, "It didn't feel like love to me."

They strolled in silence. The pause before Gary's observation had been so considered. It wasn't about letting the noisy bus go by, Binnie thought; he had taken a moment to decide whether to say something or whether that would be inappropriate meddling. That was such a Gary thing: *when is it my place to intervene*, he always seemed to be wondering? Too hands on: meddling. Too hands off: heartless. He was like the Goldilocks of inter-personal relationships.

Did Ellen love Binnie? Did Binnie love Ellen? Were they truly friends? The summer after graduation, on another long meander in the city, Ellen had confessed to Binnie that she'd auditioned to be a sushi model. They'd just seen an Off Broadway show, a birthday gift from

Ellen's parents. Outside the theater, they drifted south. The crowd transformed from camera-toting gawkers to drunken Bridge and Tunnel people. Lower order beings, Binnie thought. Then wished upon herself a terrible fate, for lightning to strike her down, to be mauled by a garbage truck.

A man in a baseball cap stumbled out of a bar and leered at Ellen's cleavage. They rushed past his red-rimmed eyes. Wandered from Midtown to the Far West Side, grit in the viscous air sticking to their sweaty skin, sunset a dusty white.

On that desolate street, Ellen mentioned the gig.

"What's a sushi model?" Binnie asked. She imagined Ellen in a tuna costume waving a sign on a street corner.

"Well, first you wax your entire body, " said Ellen.

"Uh-huh..."

"Then they rub ice all over you to cool down the skin."

Goose pimples prickled Binnie's arms.

"Then they drape your body with sushi and people eat it off your body, for, I don't know, $200 a pop?"

"And you're naked?"

"Well, they put flowers in strategic places."

Ellen didn't make the cut. Binnie thought her Rubensqueness would have been a plus: more room for sushi. But her hips didn't jut out in the right way to allow for the artful drapery of pink and red and white slabs of salmon and tuna and squid. Ellen appeared sheepish in that moment. Binnie should have hugged her.

They'd headed back to Seventh Avenue, stopped in front of the Fashion Institute of Technology. The window displayed outsized suits—full-body armor, really—made of human hair, bulbous pockets of sewn fabric, recycled sweaters, and wings fashioned from black trash bags and cheap wire hangers. Black netting covered the face, a fencing mask. *Sound Suits*, the sign said. She pictured herself lying on a cold metal table as business people with expense accounts maneuvered chopsticks around her naked body, picking raw fish off waxed, iced skin. She contemplated the heat of the Sound Suits, the weight of hair and wool. The safety and suffocation. How much she would like such a suit.

But Binnie *had* tried to hug her, hadn't she? She recalled raising her arms, Ellen putting up her hands, saying, *it's too hot*. Or had she imagined that scenario and rejected hugging her before Ellen could reject her? She hated that she couldn't remember.

Binnie now said to Gary, "Maybe I should take a little break from Ellen."

"That's probably a good idea."

Her breath caught. She wanted to reverse course and defend Ellen. Had Gary always disliked her?

But he wasn't wrong. Ellen, Binnie decided, was poison for her, at least right now. The Inquisition on her couch, the relish in her eyes. An eagerness for Binnie to give up her art and be a nothing (oblivion beats mediocrity) or else ascend to ranks of the astronomically famous, so that together at galleries far and wide they'd shimmer. The in-between was just too horrible to behold.

Binnie needed to protect herself. Gary sensed that. Invisible antennae sprang from his head, picking up on all kinds of emotional radio waves.

They trekked down Amsterdam, then across 57th. The streets were fairly deserted, but not in a creepy post-apocalyptic way. It was a clear night. You could even see a couple stars. No, one was a planet. Polaris and Venus. Binnie snuggled into her wool coat and big fluffy scarf. Gary's nose turned pink in the wind. He shivered and she rubbed his shoulder. She thought he might turn his head to kiss her, but he only said thanks and continued to shiver in her embrace, and she wondered if he even liked her, wondered why she bothered.

As they turned south on First Avenue, he said, "My parents are getting a divorce."

"Oh! I'm so sorry."

"It's all right. It's not a surprise." She rubbed his arm. "Well. It's not all right." She squeezed him. "I guess I take issue with people who break promises. I guess I'm stubborn that way." Even if things aren't working? Was that where *it didn't feel like love* came from? She pictured his house in suburban Kansas City. A ranch house or a split-level or a bungalow. A driveway with a netless basketball hoop. "He bought a bar without telling her, he thought it would be the best surprise ever. She threw him out." His mom wrapped up in a blanket on the sofa, drinking hot cider, contemplating her Miss Kansas City tiara in a glass cabinet. "They fought like lunatics. They were always doing crazy things like that. Impulsive things."

So Gary always kept his feet on the ground. Head down, nose to the grindstone. "I know it's for the best."

Binnie kissed him on the cheek.

At her door, his cold nose close, he said, "Thank you for listening."

"Of course," she said. They hugged. A real hug. Not angled away. She wondered about the timing. Whether to kiss him for real. The need for warmth. His full lips near enough to brush. As she pulled away, she asked, "Are you okay to go home? It's so late." She didn't exactly want to invite him up in a salacious way. But she worried.

"Oh, I'm fine," he said, focusing on a spot over her shoulder, clearly not fine. The kiss moment passed, and yet they lingered. "Election night," he said. "You, me, a bar in Brooklyn."

Binnie's chest sparkled. She gave him another big wet smack on the cheek before going upstairs. *Text me when you're home safe*, she texted him, feeling a little too motherly. She fell asleep with the phone on her sternum and woke forty-five minutes later to its little buzzing chirp, its red glow: *home safe*.

❖ ❖ ❖

On Tuesday, the office atmosphere brightened.

"Good morning! Did you vote?" was the refrain until lunch. On all computers, news websites were continually refreshed.

At six o'clock sharp, Binnie, brimming with hope, was on that train to Brooklyn. She and Gary dined at the cavernous old Mexican place on Fifth Avenue that now seemed out of place beside the la di da likes of Al Di La. Afterward they moved from crowded bar to crowded bar, Rachel Maddow on every screen, impossible to hear over the din of everybody who seemed to be in exactly their demographic, until they squeezed into a new cocktail lounge practically in the Gowanus Canal. A handsome young pianist sporting a bow tie played schmaltzy patriotic tunes. Closed captioning scrolled on all the televisions and, as if it were New Year's, signs promised champagne at the stroke of victory.

Conversation was limited to murmurs of state names and meaningful glances.

"Alabama."

"Kansas."

"Rhode Island!"

"Texas."

"Wisconsin!"

"Oh-hi-ooo! Oh-hi-ooo! Oh-hi-oooooooooo!"

Binnie ordered two flutes when victory seemed imminent. When Rachel Maddow finally announced Obama's projected win, people drained their champagne and then ran to the streets and hollered, as if all society's problems were finally, irrevocably solved. Gary and Binnie ran with them, and Binnie, full of some unexpected vital force, took Gary in her arms, dipped him like the sailor from "V-J Day in Times Square," and gave him a big meaty kiss on the lips.

In her mind, a grand chord sounded. Still holding him, she stopped kissing him, studied his face. His eyes were most definitely sparkling. They kissed again on the corner as cars sped up and down Fourth Avenue, swerved dangerously around corners, horns blaring. Binnie's imaginary brass band sounded again, louder and richer, metallic, victorious.

The walk to Gary's took on a jaunty pace. Laughing people spilled out of every bar. Buoyant, balloon-like. He slipped an arm around her waist and her belly fluttered. She pressed her side into his and it fluttered again.

A toy store occupied the ground floor of Gary's building. In its darkened window, pale dolls grinned. Cars zoomed up and down Seventh Avenue honking, passengers leaning out their windows, howling.

Mousetraps dotted the stairwell. They dashed upstairs, skipping around them. Kissed and kissed and kissed. Gently, Binnie bit Gary's earlobe. Laughed. Put her finger to her lips as she pulled him along, as if to shush herself, as if to tell him not to climb the stairs with his body's weight, afraid to disturb his roommates.

He lived in a three-bedroom railroad with five others. One of the roommates essentially lived in a walk-in closet. The apartment was dark, save a light over the kitchen sink, which brimmed with plates encrusted with burnt crumbs and shredded cheese. The avenue's street lamps streamed orange-yellow into the living room, where the thick windows muffled the night's revelry. On the rolled-down metal shutters of an empty shop across the street, someone was spray-painting a blue-and-red portrait of Obama.

"Get a load of that," said Binnie.

Gary turned her chin toward him. They kissed more.

"I really like you," Binnie said into his neck. He squeezed her around the waist.

"Me too. You."

Footsteps echoed up the stairs, to the door. Before they could be intruded upon, she pulled him to his darkened bedroom, gingerly navigating the amorphous path from door to bed, which Binnie knew was lined with all manner of stuff. Their coats slipped to the floor as they reached for one another, pressed against one another, fell on the bed entwining limbs. Clothes fumbled off after awkward unbuttonings and unzippings. They dived under the comforter, heat-seeking, chest to chest, belly to belly, hips to hips.

# Chapter Four

THEY FELL INTO a comfortable habit of seeing each other every other day. A week later, they were snuggled in Binnie's bed, laptop open to bootleg SNL on YouTube. She nuzzled his neck, took in his warm nutmeg scent.

"Are you ever going to unpack that bag?" he asked, nodding at the hulking black garbage bag under her worktable.

Her assemblage supplies. They'd been parked there since her move, through Election Day, through the rosy fog of Gary. She didn't want him to see what was inside. She closed up the bag whenever he was over. Until she made them part of a coherent, complete piece, the collected objects were like internal organs outside of a body. Oozing their uselessness on the operating table.

Olsen's eye shard was in there, inert. It occurred to her that a clear garbage bag full of silicone hearts and lungs might make for a disturbing piece. A jolt of excitement came with that thought, the idea to diverge from dream boxes. She could get life-size models from a medical supply company, figure out how best to cast molds. But working with silicone—would the fumes be worse than her glues? In school, they'd worn masks. At Ruby's, the windows allowed for a cross-breeze. The two-window studio was trickier. Plus, what did it mean to choose hearts and lungs? Would that catch Alexis's attention? Not without more of a story. She should articulate more of the meaning for herself before going gonzo on silicone, which she hadn't touched since school. *Don't rush*, she urged herself, despite hearing Ellen's *shit or get off the pot* echoing in her mind.

"Yes. Eventually. Not now." She pressed her cheek to Gary's shoulder, and he caressed her head. She let the familiar skits wash over her like a warm bath.

Hearts and lungs. Hearts and lungs. Hearts and lungs.

She breathed deep and sighed.

Work picked up. "People can't resist lawsuits for long," Beatrice said. It was six o'clock on a Friday and they weren't going anywhere anytime soon.

The hall elevator dinged and the door swung open, but Madeline was gone for the day. She never stayed late; she was the only one in the office with young kids.

A woman called in a tremulous voice, "Hello?" She poked her head around the divider between reception and the rest of the office. Long hair, dark and straight, an elegant sharp face in the tradition of Kate Moss.

"Oh, Beatrice," Georgina said, blushing. "Could you help me?" A little black dress clung to her swimmer's body. In the conference room, Beatrice finished zipping up the back as if that were in any way her job. "We're seeing *La Damnation de Faust*," Georgina called over her shoulder.

"Mm," Beatrice said.

Capra tossed on a scarf and coat and escorted Georgina out, his hand at her elbow.

After the door slammed shut, Rick said, "That—"

"Wasn't his wife," Beatrice said.

"Nor his daughter," Binnie said. The front door muffled Capra's words but not his anger. Binnie wondered if he had turned classic Capra red. The elevator dinged.

"She worked at Lehman," Beatrice said, as if that explained anything.

"Not anymore," Rick said.

"No," said Beatrice.

"Maybe she lost her mind," Rick said.

"Oh," said Binnie.

Everyone shrugged. A wave of dark glee at the drama further exposed surged and departed. It was interesting that Binnie and Beatrice knew who Georgina was, but not Rick. He tapped his pen on the cubicle wall, contemplating something that amused him.

Capra's wife was in big pharma. She'd gotten him on the experimental drug that saved his life. Classic Capra red was a healthy hue, like a tomato warm in the sun. Maybe he was *too* healthy now? Go forth and enjoy youth before you're truly dead?

Binnie returned to her redactions. Maybe Capra's wife approved, she mused. But if that was the case, why would he be so flustered at Georgina's appearance in the office?

Thanksgiving glowed on the horizon. The holiday party at the gallery came ever closer. Her only progress had been circular thinking, a regular rejection of ideas, a deepening self-loathing, and a dread of rent coming due. Her overtime income from the trial had disappeared fast and she was getting sick of ramen or bagels for dinner.

One Thursday night, she paced her studio, which at first had been refreshingly cool compared to Ruby's place but now was just cold. From the rickety futon to the two windows looking down on First Avenue to her worktable to the grimy sea-foam kitchenette she went, pained fingertips tucked under her arms. "Infection" sat on the floor beside the worktable, the little boy in it imploring her to come back from the kitchenette and do better. Tomorrow night she would see Gary. Tonight, she needed to sit at that table and *work*.

She rifled through the box of materials. What about the cutout of Putin and the cutout of the Marlboro Man? Put them together in a suggestive manner? They could be almost kissing, like in that Berlin Wall mural. She paper-clipped them together and pushed them to the upper corner of her table.

What about the dried peonies? They were delicate, fragile. Something without a blatant message—just wonder. She pulled out the dismantled Swan Lake music box and let her eyes unfocus while she thought. Put one flower on the tines, one beside the gears, one to the side of the knobbly cylinder, forming a triangle.

From time to time she could hear the man across the hall cackle until he coughed up a loogie. *You'll catch your death*, Arlene would say, if she knew how cold the studio was. "Peony Triangle" had a certain appeal, suggested a connection to the Bermuda Triangle. What did peonies represent, anyway? Careful not to fall in their trap! She jotted notes in her sketch pad and returned the materials to their place, feeling she'd made a millimeter of progress.

Saturday afternoon, after Gary left, she and her neighbor opened their doors at the same time, both holding bags of trash. The old man blinked at Binnie, sizing her up in much the same way his estranged wife the landlady had.

"After you," he said, finally. He'd left his door open a crack. He appeared to be in the middle of watching an infomercial on vegetable slicers. It was in that moment that Binnie remembered where she'd seen the old man before: in Union Square, sitting on a plastic milk crate demonstrating carrot peelers.

When they got to the curb, the landlady opened her window on the third floor and poked her head out. "Keep it down, *Carl*," she said, even though they hadn't been talking. Gingerly he took the metal trash can cover from Binnie and brought it down with a zealous crash.

❖ ❖ ❖

The Monday before Thanksgiving, Baxter approached Binnie's cubicle. "D'you do something different with your hair?"

Binnie patted her curls, as if to make sure she hadn't gone bald, having tugged all the hair out in her anguished ruminations. "No?"

"It looks good." Before she could say thanks he added, "There's a special gift for you in the file room."

"Oh?"

"Box of PanCorp docs to sort."

He grinned, awkwardly. She imagined the Beaux Arts bank of "Black Hole," roof caved in, plaster avalanching onto white marble. A wax doll in a pinstripe suit would peer up at the wreckage with goggling eyes. Perhaps a caption, a line of dialogue for the doll. Baxter's inane question about Olsen's shattered glass eye: *think they can put it back together?* She tried to jot down the idea before it evaporated. The wax, she realized, was inspired by the voodoo doll in *The Witches of Eastwick*. Was it Susan Sarandon who stuck in the pins?

"Hey, Bob," said Beatrice from her cube. "Your policy rider's all set."

Baxter sighed like something heavy had been lifted off him, put his palm to his chest, and thanked her.

In the file room, Binnie crouched over the PanCorp box, taking in the light stink of dusty papers and metal filing cabinets. The muffled sound of Baxter singing seeped through his closed door. She spied him through his window. He'd picked up the baseball bat he kept by his credenza, practicing his batting stance and swing, rolling his shoulders. He tossed the bat into one hand and held it like a microphone.

"Come aboard," he crooned, "we're expecting you..."

He bobbed his head like a hammy lounge singer, pacing back and forth. He leaned sideways. Why was he in such a good mood all of a sudden?

She dug through the thick files and thought of sick days at home as a kid, watching reruns of *The Love Boat* and sipping her mom's best stab at Jewish penicillin: hot chicken soup plopped from a can and garnished with a fistful of fresh parsley.

The theme song swelled: "Yes, LOOOOOOOVE! It's LOOOOOOOOOVE! Hey-ah!" Baxter poured his feelings into the song like it was the last karaoke party on earth.

Did he really think they'd win the appeal? Binnie didn't understand much about the law, but it didn't seem a likely scenario. The judge had played favorites, so there were grounds, but the whole process would be déjà vu. Why bother?

Baxter, it struck her, had faith. At least, a certain kind of faith.

Back in the summer, two teenage Lubavitchers had showed up asking for Mr. Baxter. They'd peered out from the vestibule, pale boys sporting black wool fedoras and pais, while Madeline asked Baxter if he would see them. He almost said yes, then said no, then almost said yes again. Finally, his face darkened as he said, "Send them away." Zaiman intervened, told her let the poor boys in, it's hot out there with their black wool pants and jackets. Zaiman invited them to sit in his office, then asked Binnie to fetch some cold bottles of water. When she came in he made a point of ogling the decolletage of her summer dress, her bare summer legs. Zaiman rarely asked Binnie to fetch water for him or anyone. This was some kind of weird, gross power trip. What was he insinuating to those teenage boys? It was like he wanted to perpetuate the orthodox assumption that everyone outside their community was constantly boinking: *you too could live the life of a sex-crazed goy,* he seemed to be implying. After she brought them the water, he'd closed the door, leaned back in his seat, and flashed them a chatty smile. She hoped he wasn't asking them embarrassing questions. A few minutes later, he led them back out, accepting from them a loaf of challah. He tried to give it to Baxter; Baxter refused it.

"I should have never told them I was Jewish."

They'd intercepted him in the lobby of the building once before, asked if he was Jewish and would he like to pray with them. Baxter would have been uncomfortable with the situation. She couldn't imagine him wrapping that leather strap with the black cube around his arm and head and davening there, as people streamed by with their dress shoes clopping on the marble. Publicly reconvening with a culture he'd white-washed.

What was the mysterious black cube all about, anyway? Binnie had gone to Hebrew school and knew there was a little prayer scroll inside but still, she didn't *truly* know. It was like a miniature version of the monolith in *2001: A Space Odyssey.* Or that famous black cube of a mosque. Only you tied it to the forehead—atop the third eye?

Inside a lacquered black box, a blank mannequin head is backlit with blue LEDs. Strapped on the mannequin's forehead, the black cube. Trumpeting out of little speakers in the box's dark corners, the soundtrack from *2001*: buuuuh-Baaah-BAAAAH! Ba-BAAAAAH! DUM dum DUM dum DUM dum DUM dum. An eyelid on the cube rises. A glass iris gleams.

Was that wrong? It felt wrong. Madonna, with her study of Kabbalah and affected British accent, probably knew more than Binnie about such things, and this displeased her.

How had Baxter wriggled out of praying with those boys after he'd admitted he was, in their eyes, a lapsed Jew?

"Well, if you don't want it," Zaiman had said of the challah, "I'm making French toast tomorrow. Goes great with bacon!"

"C'mon," Baxter had said. "Be respectful."

"Half my mother's family was slaughtered in the Holocaust," Zaiman said, still holding the challah. "There is no God. I'm eating bacon."

Baxter shifted his weight from one foot to the other before disappearing into his office.

Something about Baxter's discomfort at that moment seemed connected to his general uneasiness, which had become so apparent when Harrison was on the witness stand. It was like with religion, he didn't want to admit some part of him might believe, and when it came to this case, he didn't want to admit that he didn't. His sense of duty to both cut him up in all kinds of directions.

Then there was the other grossness of the trial that Binnie couldn't begin to discuss with anyone, even though Capra himself had raised the specter before they went down to Wilmington for two weeks. What would a Delaware jury think of brash New York Jews? It didn't matter what you said, exactly. It was the accent, the manner of speaking, the look—here, Zaiman supplied his seemingly favorite adjective, "swarthy." The lead attorney on the other side, Broderick Williams, had been just as greedy as anyone on their side. Binnie knew it in her roiling, resentment-steeped liver. But he was from D.C., just shy of the Mason-Dixon line: strawberry blond, chisel-faced, patrician in the most WASPy way Binnie could imagine. You have to care about money but without caring about money in the Old Money way, she had thought, as she watched some of the jury members gawp at Williams with fanboy admiration.

The workday dragged on. A pinprick floater warned Binnie of an oncoming migraine. Shutting her eyes, she willed herself to relax. She realized she hadn't seen Paul all day and went to peep into his tiny office. His porkpie hat and congeniality might cheer her up. Paul was a part-time attorney, part-time filmmaker. How he made that work, Binnie wasn't sure, but it gave her hope. And he sported rosy cheeks her Aunt Ruby would have surely pinched. He'd been the one person in the office with a whiff of artistic sensibility, the one person who, upon meeting, she thought might become a friend.

But there was no Paul, no porkpie hat, no cheeks. His office had been wiped clean of any trace of him. She fidgeted in the hall, much the same way as Baxter had. She shook herself, as if to shake off his squeamish influence, and decisively approached Beatrice.

"Is Paul...gone?"

For a millisecond, Beatrice's eyes darted in Rick's direction, then refocused on Binnie.

"Unfortunately, we had to terminate his contract."

"Oh. Why?"

Beatrice's head tilted as her left eyebrow arched.

"Sorry," said Binnie. Another floater drifted over Beatrice's head.

In the copy room, a few minutes later, Rick stopped slicing backs on the paper cutter.

"It was determined that he wasn't pulling his weight," he informed Binnie. Strips of blue paper fluttered into the recycling bin from the office guillotine.

"But Thanksgiving week?"

"You and I, without law degrees, are just as capable. He was expensive." Rick shrugged. "Dems da breaks."

"Da breaks are harsh."

The abyss between Binnie's pay and Rick's resurfaced in her mind. *What a steal,* they must have thought. Peter Pan slot machine coins clattered in a deluge accompanied by bells and whistles. The migraine aura narrowed her vision.

The water boiler on the kitchen counter gurgled and clicked. Rick made himself a cup of tea and offered Binnie one. She demurred. He fished around for something behind the tea boxes. A shiny candy that fit in her palm, with a cartoon turkey on the wrapper.

"Happy Thanksgiving, you crazy kid," Rick said.

Alone in the room, with just the hum of the Xerox machine and the hot sigh of the water burbling, Binnie contemplated the foil turkey. The red Paralegal binder on her desk held a series of departure memos, dated a year or two apart from one another. That was just the paralegals who'd quit; she also knew of a handful who'd been fired. Rick said, triumphantly, that he'd caught one guy snorting coke in the bathroom. (Good thing he hadn't come to Delaware, she supposed.) But there were more mundane reasons for the high turnover. Too many sloppy mistakes. A missed deadline. A lie on a resume. And the people who could do this work competently were a dime a dozen. Not dumb, sure, but not so special either.

The shiny orange and brown wrapper crinkled between her fingers. Turkey wattles were so gross. So vulnerable. The migraine began, a rusted rod drilling through the left side of her skull. She ripped open the foil, splitting the cartoon bird's head in half, and paused before sinking her teeth into its chocolate neck, collapsing the delicate shell into gelatinous marshmallow.

❖ ❖ ❖

Thanksgiving dinner was at Arlene and Albert's. Arlene asked if Binnie wanted to invite any friends who might be Thanksgiving orphans. Against her better judgment, Binnie invited Gary over to meet her parents, barely three weeks into their relationship. Gary was not flying home for the holiday; it was never worth it, he said, for just four days. And he couldn't choose one parent over another during the divorce.

"My dad's going to be in a motel," he said, voice brittle.

"You want to be with him?"

"I can't."

Anyway, he'd get a bonus for working the phones on Black Friday, offering fifty- and sixty-something-year-old women the cosmetics and wine club gift packages first thing in the morning.

"Okay, but fair warning about my family's food—"

"I love canned cranberry sauce. I love the way it jiggles."

"No deep-fried turkey. No brining. No Julia Child butter massages."

"I *love* dry turkey."

Gary waited in front of her parents' building, holding a casserole. He'd gotten there before her but didn't want to go inside alone.

"I walked around the block," he said.

"I do that sometimes," she said, kissing him over her sloshing bowl of cranberry sauce. "What did you bring?"

"Brisket. I can't have Thanksgiving without it."

"My dad's gonna love you."

Inside, the steam heat clanged away, the warmth a shock compared to the tundra Binnie had become accustomed to in her studio. She peeled off her sweater and rolled up the sleeves of her turtleneck.

"Everything's almost done," Arlene called from the kitchen. She came out with silverware and plastic place-mats and "festive" paper napkins from Ikea and shook

Gary's hand, giving his eyes an intense inspection. Her millisecond-long examination of his soul seemed to lead to approval. "Very nice to meet you, young man. I'm sure Binnie must think the world of you."

"Mom," Binnie said. "Let me help you set the table."

Albert rose from the couch and clapped Gary on the shoulder. "I hope you don't mind if the game isn't on. I'm not much of a football fan."

Gary spent the occasional weekend afternoon at a divey sports bar on Fifth Avenue, where crusty old men started nursing Budweisers at 10:00 a.m. and snoozed over empty bottles into the early evening. "Me neither," he said, smiling

Everyone oohed and ahhed over Gary's brisket, a juicy slab of beef slathered in tomato paste. Arlene passed around boiled Brussels sprouts as Albert carved the turkey. Binnie plopped mashed potatoes in her plate and Gary's and drowned both in gravy.

"Gimme some more of that brisket sauce," Albert said, "and I'll put it right on my turkey."

The party sawed at meat and chewed on overcooked vegetables.

"So? Tell us," said Albert. "How's work?"

"Ugh," said Binnie. "I don't know." She pushed some turkey around her plate. Mashed potatoes buried the meat. "I kind of want to quit."

Arlene raised an eyebrow. "Why."

"I don't know. Nothing bad happened to me, it's not like that, but Delaware was just...*gross*." The turkey emerged from under the potatoes and she splatted it into the pile again, unsure of how to explain. Stopped herself from stabbing harder. Couldn't let Gary see her act like a whiny baby. Words tumbled out anyway, in a mealy-mouthed despair. "Lawyers are gross. Everything is gross."

Arlene's face fell. She opened the rare bottle of Merlot they drank on holidays and poured everyone a glass, taking time to gather energy before she spoke.

"Are you really going to quit? Do you have a solid plan? You know, without Ruby's apartment, you'll be in a real pickle."

"It's okay, Arlene," Albert said, delicately placing more white meat on everyone's plates. No one seemed comfortable grabbing a turkey leg. Breast meat was more genteel. Binnie suppressed the urge to rip off a drumstick, dunk it in the gravy boat, and devour it Medieval Times–style. "Let's just talk about nicer things. You never told us much about Wilmington. Was the city nice?"

Binnie shook her head and stared at her plate. The neatly mosaicked lobby of the DuPont came to mind, with its photographs of famed guests—presidents and kings and Henry Kissinger. "The Hotel DuPont was pretty. But really, there's not much to see." She pushed the same piece of turkey around in a slurry of gravy, cranberry sauce, and Brussels sprout juice. She *had* seen the top of Joe Biden's silvery head at the train station, with a hefty entourage buzzing around him, which was kind of neat. But somehow it didn't seem worth noting aloud.

"So, Mr. and Mrs. Greenson," Gary interjected, lightly tapping Binnie's elbow. "How did you two meet?"

"Ohhh," they cooed together.

"Let me tell you," said Albert. "We were in high school."

"Midwood."

"And there was an all-school egg drop competition—"

"—not like the soup!"

"He knows what I mean. Right?"

"Like in a physics class, right?"

"Right," said Albert, a little check-mark of approval in his voice.

"And I had devised a very pretty parachute out of a handkerchief and dental floss," said Arlene. "And Al had done something else. What was it, Al?"

"Ball bearings. A paper cup bottomed with ball bearings."

"And my egg landed on his egg," said Arlene, slamming one fist onto the other. "Plop." She flattened her bottom hand. "Crack." Then she dusted her hands together as if that explained the rest of their relationship. "Happily ever after."

"Wow," said Gary.

Arlene and Albert eyed each other over the table. Well-masticated turkey slid down Binnie's gullet. On a display shelf behind Gary sat the stuffed crocodile Binnie had gotten from her parents' get-away weekend to the now-shuttered Peg & Hook casino, part of Peter Pan's suite of bankrupt businesses. The radiator hissed.

During the trial, while Williams had picked at financial minutiae to illustrate PanCorp's wrongdoing in his steady, sober manner, with none of the self-interrupting drama Zaiman favored—the sale of a Caribbean cruise liner featuring acrobatic swashbuckling, a prime Las Vegas casino with a high-rollers' club called the Plunder Room, a New Orleans hotel with a wildly popular restaurant called Tink's Table— a craving for deep fried Oreos had crept onto Binnie's tongue. Only Atlantic City's best. She'd eat a bucket of hot cookies like it was popcorn, cram her cheeks with them like a chipmunk. She imagined Joseph Cornell eating them too, forlornly on the Jersey shore, then got another dream box idea: inside a big glass bottle, Victorian illustrations of swashbuckling pirates and Lost Boys, tussling on a ship. Behind them, at the center of the composition, clambering aboard from the sea: Ursula the Sea Witch, the Disney version's face pasted on a Japanese woodblock print of an octopus body. But in the middle she'd have Venus of Willendorf tits— maybe it would be an old photograph or old anthropological drawing—and the octopus tentacles would be poised to grab pirate and Lost Boy alike and press them to her bosom—and smother them.

Binnie's plate was empty. She pulled at the top of her turtleneck. "I need some air," she said.

"Everything okay?" asked Arlene.

"Just feeling warm," she said, pushing herself away from the table. Stifled, in fact. The heat prickled her skin. She wanted to give her whole body a shake. The cooler air of the imitation granite hall granted a small reprieve. She stomped down the stairs and out to Ocean Parkway into the bracing cold. Gary followed.

"Your mom asked me to bring you your coat."

Binnie laughed. "Of course she did." She took her coat but didn't put it on.

"Aren't you cold?"

"Aren't you hot?"

"Is something wrong?"

Binnie gulped air. "It's just a little too much right now. I can't—I can't do what they want me to do. I want to live how *I* want to live. I can't do the same meaningless thing day in and day out. I'm gonna die leaving nothing of consequence." She opened her eyes; they'd snapped closed on the last sentence.

Gary appeared pained. He scratched the back of his neck like he couldn't decide whether to hug her or recommend therapy.

"I'm sorry," Binnie said.

Immediately after apologizing, she wondered if she should not have apologized. There was nothing wrong with her desire to do something of consequence as compared to what Arlene, Albert, and Gary did. She thought Gary was deeply stuck, she admitted to herself. His low pay meant trying to get as many hours as possible, and between that and the long commute he never seemed to have the time to find something better. He was deeply in debt from college and worked a sales job that any high school graduate would be fine at; the degree offered the tiny solace of maybe one day becoming the middle manager of a business he couldn't care less about. Binnie couldn't figure out what Gary was passionate about beyond his vague sense of wanting to do something good for the world. He always lit up around the children clambering on the shiny orange seats of the F train; she imagined he'd make a great school teacher. His student debt would certainly not be fixed by *that* career change.

Cars whooshed off the Prospect Expressway and down Ocean Parkway. She craned her neck back. The full moon shone through the bare branches of a thin locust tree—Betty Smith's tree, of *A Tree Grows in Brooklyn* fame. Binnie imagined a campaign for it. *The locust tree: thriving despite circumstances since 1943.*

Gently, Gary said, "They just want to make sure you have a plan. That's all."

"I know. A soulless plan. A plan of drudgery." She focused on the moon through the branches.

"I don't think that's fair."

"Everything they expect is too normal. It's unreal and dead."

"That sounds...really dramatic, Binnie. Are you sure you're not overreacting?"

She wasn't about to ask if he'd read *The Bell Jar* or explain the feeling of a glass dome descending over everything. She didn't want him to become alarmed at the implication of the reference, if he knew it, or at the oddity of the explanation, if he didn't. Maybe it was a thing you just got or didn't get. "I just want to live a life that feels alive."

"Doesn't everybody?"

"I guess."

"Binnie, do you respect what I do?" It came out fast, not one of his long-considered utterances like when he'd suggested a break from Ellen. It was a turn she didn't want the conversation to take, but it was her own damn fault that it was going that way.

"You are not your job." She scuffed her shoe into a pile of foliage. "Does it bother you when I buy you dinner?"

His cheeks flushed. "What does *that* mean?"

"Withdrawn." She crunched the leaves. "I don't know. I'm confused."

Gary glanced up; Binnie followed his gaze. A couple carried two casseroles into another building, giggling as they murmured to each other, the woman's lipstick pleasingly dark and thick. A spiky chestnut fell from a nearby tree.

Gary's face smoothed. "Binnie," he said, finally. "*You* make me feel alive." His tone suggested a desire to mend the situation, even though he was the one who'd been hurt.

"I do?"

Gary nodded and held out his arms. It felt good, at first, the notion that she could give someone else a feeling of aliveness. And Gary deserved it. She leaned into the magnetic pull of his embrace, even though a hug was the last thing she wanted. It didn't feel any more freeing than her parents' overheated apartment. She would rather they sprint into the dark together, as quickly as possible. She grabbed his arm.

"Let's go for a walk. We'll come back for dessert."

"Should we tell your parents?"

"We'll be quick."

She yanked him toward the bridge over the expressway, then toward Prospect Park.

"Where are we going?"

"Ducks or horses?"

"What?"

"You choose: ducks or horses. Then we go back for dessert."

"Okay...horses."

"Excellent choice." Instead of entering the park, she veered into the pocket of Windsor Terrace where the tiny Kensington Stables lived. They stood outside the locked-up, white wooden doors.

"Do you want to go horseback riding sometime, when they're open?" asked Gary.

"Shh," said Binnie. She closed her eyes. She wanted to hear a horse snort. There was a quiet scuffle inside, hooves shifting on hay. She smiled. "Poor horses."

Gary squeezed her hand. She imagined a horse fluttering its lips. Imagined a dark, small-windowed dream box in which you could just barely make out equine silhouettes, the gleams in horses' eyes. A recorded scuffle, so faint and irregularly timed that you could never be sure you really heard it. A scent of manure, so faint you'd have to question your detection of it. She hadn't thought to include scent in her work. She thrilled at the idea. From *shit or get off the pot* to actual horse shit.

She kissed Gary's cheek meatily. They hugged, belly to belly. Now that they'd run into the woods, now that her blood pumped more vigorously, the hug felt right.

Outside her parents' building, a rangy, mottled cat skimmed their legs. "You're still working on something to show Alexis, right?"

A little of the fresh air went out of her. "Yes, definitely," she said, despite the sensation that she had very little to show for herself.

Only after her second helping of dessert did it occur to her that people might not want to *purchase* art that literally smelled like shit.

# Chapter Five

ON THE FIRST of December, Capra unveiled a pyramid of heritage Asian pears, each fruit cradled in a foam lattice. He cooed as if they were rare gems. Thus began an onslaught of holiday gifts: chocolate truffles and sugar cookies and sea salt caramels from the south of France.

Hourly, Binnie devoured treats. Occasionally she spied Baxter doing the same, alone in the kitchen. Face drooping, shoulders slumped, eyes lusterless. Gold and silver foil littering the counter. Zaiman hectored him; his clients were losers, criminals. Baxter waved him away, let the taunts fall on his back on his way to the sugar. One time he noticed Binnie standing there. He straightened his posture and forced a smile that, eventually, seemed genuine. She couldn't help but think this was a transformation he performed regularly, not just at work but at home for his college-aged daughter Becca, a freshman at Tufts. He'd grimaced over a Pepto Bismol tablet on the

Acela to Wilmington, telling Zaiman of Becca's plan to spend winter break skiing in Switzerland. Binnie had met her over the summer. A happy-go-lucky teen with diamond stud earrings and vocal fry. Probably not someone who noticed the subtleties of smiles.

❖ ❖ ❖

On Saturday morning, Binnie's phone vibrated.

*Long time. Coming tonight?*

Gary snuggled up to Binnie. "Who's that?"

Binnie flipped her phone shut. "Ellen."

"What'd she want?"

"The holiday party is tonight."

"Oh, yeah. Do you...want to go?"

"I thought I was taking a break from Ellen."

"You should probably go."

Binnie flipped open her phone again. Flipped it shut. Flipped it open. "Probably should." *See you there,* she typed. As soon as she hit send, her stomach turned.

"I won't bring anything to show Alexis, though," she said. "It would be stupid and presumptuous. Like, why would she look at my stuff? She'll be busy with the party."

"Just go check it out and be seen. I'll be your arm candy."

Binnie sighed. "Fine."

"Now how about you let me distract you?"

They sank back under the covers in a tangle of limbs.

❖ ❖ ❖

In the bathroom, Binnie sharpened her eyeliner and applied it to the vulnerable rims of her eyes, adjusting wobbly lines into smoky smudges. Somehow, she reflected, Ellen knew how to rub Binnie's face in it without ever knowing what Binnie's *it* was.

They'd grown up in wildly different versions of New York City. Binnie had understood that the first time she met Ellen's parents at a reception at *their* gallery, soon after graduation. She'd been standing beside a video of a nude woman rolling around in yogurt and Vaseline on a tarp, spliced with images of a piglet nuzzling an absurdly red apple. Ellen's parents were making the rounds; Binnie overcompensated for her shyness by practically lunging at them. Chilly and aloof, they'd warmed up to her when learning that Ellen knew Binnie from their alma mater. Cooed, "Pleased to meet you." They were white-haired and angular, nothing like curvy Ellen. An edgy version of the farmer couple in *American Gothic*. Binnie worried they'd always associate her with the rooting piglet and the squish of petroleum jelly.

Ellen's parents had, of course, helped her get the job at the gallery in West Chelsea. She was open about it, didn't mind getting help from them. That's how you survived in this city, she said. Bootstraps are bullshit. She'd expounded upon this before offering to get Binnie an interview. Although Binnie was struggling to make ends meet with sporadic work at the time, she'd demurred, not wanting to put herself in the position of fetching Ellen's morning coffee or oatmeal or *pain au chocolat*. Being at Ellen's beck and call was not an option, not if she wanted to keep her as a friend. Someone she could talk to frankly, despite everything. Ellen knew too much about Binnie and Binnie knew too much about Ellen, via the deep confessional mode of their shared past, rooted in midnight instant-message chats about the mean things they'd done in middle and high school—Binnie had once stitched a voodoo doll of a girl she disliked; Ellen spread the news of a friend's loss of virginity to her entire social circle—or about bad college dates.

> Ellie123: *He pushed your head where*
> Binster: *I should make revenge art*
> Ellie123: *Yeah!*
> Binster: *A rubber mold of his head set on a spike*
> Ellie123: *...*
> Binster: *Outside his dorm window before he wakes*
> Ellie123: *Your sick lolololol*

She rinsed anti-frizz serum off her fingers and wiped off the lipstick she'd just applied, leaving behind the faintest stain.

❖ ❖ ❖

Medieval chorales rang through the dim gallery; visitors chattered above their hum. The buzz that night surrounded a series of bluish mottled paintings of a slinky, sandy-haired woman lying in an old claw-footed bathtub, empty of water. Its coating flaked. In each iteration, faint markings on her arm or leg or shoulder suggested a vagina. *Where's Waldo?* for genitalia. The music and paintings together suggested to Binnie a sex cult, something out of the world of *Rosemary's Baby*.

They sipped prosecco and searched the crowd for Ellen.

"I'm sure there's a secret penis," a woman in puce said, in passing.

"The secret penis is the viewer," replied a man in a bulbous Comme des Garçons jacket.

"The Male Gaze": A skull with two silicone penises bobbling out of the eye sockets. Binnie bit her tongue and peered down at her black boots to stop herself from laughing.

"There she is," Gary said. Across the room, Ellen, all in black, stood at the elbow of a woman of Amazonian stature in a vermilion sheath dress that accentuated her healthy bone structure. Thick black hair, straight and sleek, hung down to her waist. Rapunzel quality—you could scale a building on that hair. The man in the bulbous coat pulled the Amazon away from Ellen. Binnie and Gary gravitated toward her.

"He's totally buying the whole series," Ellen murmured, eyes sparkling.

Binnie tilted her head toward the Amazon. "Is that the artist?"

"That's my boss."

"Oh!" The patrician, fifty-something, Susan Sontag doppelganger version of Alexis vanished from Binnie's mind. "Where's the artist?"

Ellen turned. In another corner of the room stood

the slinky woman of the paintings, wearing a black knit cap and a slouchy sweater that fell off one shoulder. The Amazon was now introducing the bulbous-coated man to her, and he was shaking her one hand in his meaty two. The Amazon was all smiles. Binnie drained her glass and felt flushed.

The Amazon moved on with a toothy grin. Ellen grabbed Binnie by the arm.

"Alexis," she blurted. "I want you to meet my good friend Binnie. You should see her work sometime."

Alexis's eyebrow arched, giving Binnie a swift appraisal that felt wholly different from the one Arlene had subjected Gary to. Binnie wished she had given more thought to her outfit beyond a boxy sweater and her "nice" jeans. "Charmed. And what do you do?" She asked it hurriedly, seemed eager to move on.

"Dioramas? Like, uh, assemblages, that sort of thing." Binnie's face burned.

"Charming. Come in sometime, show me something," Alexis said, handing her a card. Binnie took it and patted her purse as if to find a card of her own to give, which she did not have. Alexis had no time for this charade. A silver fox of a man with a young, intricately freckled face moved toward them.

"Excuse me," Alexis said, lightly touching Binnie's shoulder. Binnie's insides wrestled around like a hyena. "Brent!" They air-kissed. "Ellen, take Brent's coat."

Ellen winked at Binnie and they were gone. The hyena rolled around in the grass while Binnie's heart pounded in her ears. *You imbecile*, she thought. That was way too easy. Way, way too easy. Alexis had just wanted to get rid of her; why had Ellen put her on the spot?

She turned to Gary. "I think this means we can go now?"

Gary seemed disappointed to leave the party so soon. "Really?"

Binnie gave one furtive nod.

"All right. If you want." Outside, he jettisoned the disappointment. "I'm proud of you."

She stared at the card, minimalist gray with a hint of cantaloupe. *Alexis Thorne, curator.* The phone number used chic dots rather than dashes. "I didn't *do* anything."

He *tsked.* "Can we be happy, please?"

"I'm sorry. Yes. Let's celebrate! Let's get fancy cocktails."

They found a spot down the street, on the edge of the Meat Packing District, and drank pomegranate and elderflower concoctions in vintage cordial glasses, $18 each. A group of young men one table over grew rowdier with each bottle of Moet Chandon until one of them smashed his coupe glass to the gleaming white subway tile and challenged his friend to a race. The bouncer escorted them out. Through the window, Binnie and Gary watched a Ferrari and a Lamborghini screech away on the cobblestones as the remaining boys cheered from the curb.

❖ ❖ ❖

On Tuesday: zero billable work. Binnie slipped envelopes into the postage meter. It went *eeee-eeee-eeee-THUMP*. She thought about Alexis, whether to take her tossed-off invitation seriously. Ellen certainly did. She'd texted that Sunday: *First Saturday in Jan: brunch party at the gallery. Bring something.*

On her first day of work, she'd been tasked with scanning two thousand brittle pages from Capra's most esteemed client, the Hermès estate. The machine kept jamming, blinking red and honking *failure failure failure*. Elbow-deep in the ass of it, her sweaty cheek pressed to overheated plastic, she wondered how this compared to helping a cow give birth. Would she rather her arm in that kind of mysterious warmth than this kind of mysterious warmth? It would have been more spiritually rewarding, at least.

Now the fax machine, beside the postage meter, sucked sheets through its printer. A paralegal resume came through, then a cover sheet addressed to Capra from a Tennessee court and several pages of court documents. Whistling, Rick plucked them out of the tray, chucking the resume.

"Wait, are you just throwing that out?"

"You can give it to Beatrice, if you prefer. She'll throw it out."

Binnie frowned. "I'll give that court document to Capra."

"Knock yourself out."

In his office, Capra's radio voice broke into high-pitched exasperation.

"What's wrong with this new Excel?"

"There's this quote," Binnie said. "Every enhancement is also an amputation."

Capra cocked his head to the side, a quizzical expression morphing into something faintly impressed, and she felt like she'd scored a point. She handed him the fax.

"Summary judgment?" He broke out laughing, as if he'd gotten away with something. *A good lawyer knows the law*, he'd once quipped. *A great lawyer knows the judge.*

❖ ❖ ❖

In the lobby the next morning, a crowd jostled in front of the towering, pink-and-gold-ornamented Christmas tree. Binnie paused at the security desk, disturbed at what she saw. Shouting men in business suits: twenty or so of them, with arms raised, hands grasping the air. Face veins visibly pulsed throughout the tightly clustered mini-riot, while security guards and police kept the men at bay. It seemed the crowd was trying to get through to the elevators. All they were missing was torches and pitchforks. Binnie had never seen anything like it. Not in real life. It was like news footage of the New York Stock Exchange but worse, strained throats and temples on the verge of explosion, arms ready to bludgeon.

The men were not blocking the elevator bank Binnie needed, so she proceeded, giving the scene a wide berth while she rubbernecked at the agitating crowd.

Upstairs, shaken, she asked Madeline if she'd seen the

ruckus, but Madeline shook her head and said she'd come in at seven to catch up on filing.

"Let me check the news," she said, but there wasn't anything online yet.

"Fucking A," Baxter muttered, bursting through the front door.

Zaiman waved Baxter into his office, closed the door, and pulled the blinds down. Baxter's silhouette paced. A stabby conversation, voices staccato.

Capra arrived, eyes delicately leaking.

"What's happening?" Madeline asked.

"Angry investors. Downstairs. Hold my calls." He knocked on Zaiman's door and slipped inside.

Madeline's spine straightened. "Oh—ohhhh. I bet it's that hedge fund on the nineteenth floor."

It was a large firm, she explained, much bigger than Helios and Cronos, the mysterious hedge fund that resided next door to CZB. The only reason Binnie even knew about this obscure neighbor was because an energetic young woman with graying hair had introduced herself in the elevator one morning.

"I'm Priti," she'd said, shooting out her hand to shake Binnie's after they exchanged weather-related pleasantries.

"What do you do?" Binnie asked.

"I manage Cronos."

"What's that?"

"A fund of funds," she said breathlessly, almost conspiratorially, before disappearing behind the inconspicuous black door.

What's a fund of funds? Binnie wondered. Were there also funds of funds of funds? The creation myth came to mind, the one with the crust of the earth teetering upon an infinite pile of turtles. Turtles all the way down.

The sound of Zaiman flopping on his leather sofa ended the partners' meeting. Binnie wanted to ask Madeline what more she knew, but the door swung open. A moment of silence preceded the heavy step of dress shoes on carpet. Baxter yanked the Zombie out of his office for a cigarette. Binnie expected Capra to say *release the hounds.*

"Get me reservations for four at Jean-Georges," he said to Madeline. "Twelve o'clock."

"Oh-kay."

"Bernie—" Zaiman shouted from his prone position.

"Relax, will you?"

At lunchtime, the riot in the lobby dispersed, but a larger crowd of reporters with notepads, cameras, and microphones gathered outside. Binnie followed a cluster of men emerging from the elevator bank for the bottom twenty stories of the building, thinking they'd clear a path for her. First a burly, younger man went through the revolving doors, then a droopy-faced man with longish gray hair, then Binnie. The young man tried to clear a path into the crowd of journalists and cameramen. The older man hung back in the bay of the revolving door, avoiding the journalists lunging at him with questions. This meant that Binnie was stuck inside the revolving doors. She could not go backwards or forwards without the glass smacking into the older man. She imagined a doll-sized version herself in a transparent box, creepily blank-faced and pushing against a motionless door. Better yet, fill the box with pliable rubber dolls in business attire, filling the box so tight their limbs would be splayed in awkward directions, their noses smushed to the glass.

Finally the men succeeded in fighting their way out. The swarm followed them. Binnie escaped and slipped around the edge of the crowd.

"Ma'am, do you have any comments?" asked a reporter after the men slipped into a black SUV and sped off.

"Who was that?"

"Bernie Madoff," said the reporter, disappointed he didn't have a scoop.

"Who's that?"

He goggled at her. "King of the biggest Ponzi scheme in history."

The ordeal made Binnie ravenous. On the corner she devoured a gyro in ten large bites, raw onions and tsatziki sauce slopping on the sidewalk. Pigeons and seagulls alighted on these droppings, the seagulls quickly beating out the pigeons.

Back upstairs, she stopped by Madeline's desk.

"I got stuck behind Madoff in the revolving doors," she said.

"No kidding."

Madeline beckoned her over to her computer. Every news site had screaming headlines about Madoff, the Ponzi scheme, the billions of dollars lost. That morning's angry crowd had consisted of investors who'd lost money elsewhere in the economic downturn and were now trying to pull their money out of Madoff Investment Securities, but it was too late for them.

Now little birds took up the other quarters of her imagined revolving door diorama. À la Cornell's "Aviaries." A blue-feathered, ruby-throated hummingbird; a pelican in full bloat; a tawny wood pigeon—so much nicer than your average rat with wings. The birds could be the most flamboyant subjects in a stark setting of white walls and glass. Maybe it could take on a Hitchcockian flavor. *The Birds*, but gaudily colorful. Audubon, but obviously murderous.

Perhaps the door could be mechanized, so the birds would move as if in a carousel.

Or perhaps they'd be in the process of getting pulled into the gyre. Lee Bontecou's industrial constructions came to mind, laundry-conveyor-belt canvas wrangled over steel and shaped into an all-devouring mouth of overwhelming anxiety, the negative space the equivalent of Bontecou grabbing you by the collar and sucking you into darkness.

Perhaps she could reference this in "Black Hole," make them companion pieces. Birds sucked into an abyss at the top of a bank, its roof caving.

She had no shortage of ideas. The problem was completion. The problem was execution. Time. Skill. She slapped her palm on the desk, hard, startling Madeline.

"You okay?"

"Sorry—I—guess I just got mad at the scheme."

Madeline cocked her head at Binnie, but before she could say anything the phone rang and the day went on.

◈ ◈ ◈

"He'll just get a slap on the wrist," Arlene said when she called Binnie that night, panting for juicy details she couldn't get from the news.

"You really think so," Binnie said.

"It's not what I *want*, Binnie. It's what I think."

"A *shonda*," Al said.

"Of course it is," Arlene answered, putting on a more serious tone.

The next morning, Madoff was arrested in his home. That day and the next brought news of more and more victims who'd lost everything, including people who were not among the richest of the rich but desperately wanted to be, as well as a handful of universities and charitable foundations. Binnie half-expected to find some personal connection to the mess, like a friend of a friend of a friend going bankrupt or some organization that had passed through her life closing its doors, but all she found was a deep squeamishness over Madoff being Jewish.

The FBI shut down access to Madoff's offices, which occupied the seventeenth to the nineteenth floors, and were carefully combing through their files. A three-floor operation—so much larger than CZB's tiny digs. The seventeenth floor was where the money had disappeared. Investigators in windbreakers streamed in and out of the building. It was exciting if you didn't think too much about all the people who'd been screwed over.

Zaiman sat back in his office chair as Baxter lingered in his doorway, nails chewed down to stubs.

"Won't be great for the Jews," Zaiman said. Baxter dismissed Zaiman with a wave of the hand and darkened face, gallumphed out for a cigarette.

Friday morning, the partners and Beatrice held a long meeting in the conference room. The tone was somber. Binnie worried they'd announce that CZB had invested millions with Madoff. They'd all gone off the deep end, they were doomed, and Binnie had a long, illustrious future as a bag lady.

They streamed out of the conference room, revealing nothing.

Baxter and Zaiman began calling employees into Baxter's office one by one, first the Zombie—addressed as "Mr. Jones," abruptly and with a short, nervous laugh—then Rick, then Madeline. All solemn. Poker faces everywhere. Binnie grasped at her wrists; she leaned forward, broke into a cold sweat. Maybe I am getting laid off, she thought. I can't afford my studio. I cannot cannot cannot live with my parents. They are going to kill me. The ghost of Ruby will haunt me forever. Idiot! I cannot cannot cannot go to law school.

Toward the end of the day, it was finally her turn.

"Binnie, would you come and see us now?" said Baxter. An impassive expression on his face surely hid a grave situation. She grabbed a notepad and pen.

"You won't be needing that," said Zaiman.

Oh boy. All her mistakes had come to light. She had helped them lose the trial. The firm was bankrupt. She was going to lose her job, effective immediately. She'd be on a park bench with all her belongings stuffed into plastic bags from C-Town by the end of the month, muttering to her only friends, the pigeons.

Binnie settled into the chair in front of Baxter's disconcertingly neat desk. Usually a maelstrom of papers covered every inch of it.

"This is your year-end review," he said.

"*Oh,*" she almost exclaimed. She sat back, then forward. It could still be bad. Baxter thanked her for her help with the trial, praised her calm demeanor. She wanted to laugh at that. Calm? Had she missed out on a lucrative career in acting?

Caught off guard, Baxter had lately appeared damaged. If she were an expressionist, she'd paint his portrait in bruised tones and hacked at the center, like one of Francis Bacon's self-portrait distortions. But now any pain over the PanCorp loss was well hidden as he slipped into his role of evaluator. Placid, with a glint of empathy and intelligence.

"Business has been slow," he said.

Here it came. It was happening right now. She was fucked.

"So I'm sorry we can't give you a bigger bonus," he said.

The mental images of herself tumbling down a flight of stairs paused. A bonus? She'd never had a bonus. She wished he'd say again how much it was, because she'd missed it. A nice round, four-digit number, maybe something *they* would sneeze at, but not her.

Maybe she could buy a whole bunch of prosthetic eyes.

"But we're able to give you a raise, $38.5." Oh. Huh. She wasn't sure if that was a good raise or not. Couldn't they have jumped up to a bigger, rounder number? Should she say something about Rick's salary? Maybe that would be whiny. Ungrateful.

"Thank you," said Binnie, stunned. "Thank you very much." Was it okay to say Happy Hanukkah? Well, she would say it. "Happy Hanukkah."

"You too."

She tottered out of Baxter's office. Zaiman was soon behind, pulling on his coat. Capra, too, was putting on a round fur cap, somewhat Tsarist in style.

"I like your hat," Binnie said.

"Thank you," Capra said.

"It looks really warm." She considered wearing such a hat around her tundra of a studio.

"It is!"

The phone rang. Capra lingered, expectant.

Binnie answered. An agitated voice huffed into her ear.

"Bernie, please."

Her heart leapt. "Wait, who?"

"*Capra*. My husband."

Margaret hurled words like darts.

Binnie covered the mouthpiece.

"It's for you."

Capra grabbed the receiver. "Yes, yes. I know. I'm already out the door."

"..."

"I know I said that an hour ago. I have my hat on. If you hang up now, I'll be home in five minutes."

"..."

"*Yes*." He handed the phone back to Binnie. "Well, I'm off," he said, grin tight. "We have reservations tonight." Le Cirque, perhaps? La Grenouille? *Mais non*. Most likely a restaurant so cutting edge Binnie had never heard of it.

He disappeared around the reception wall, but the door did not swing open in a hurry. She heard him pause at Madeline's desk.

"Pretty happy about your bonus, eh?" he murmured.

An odd lilt in his tone.

Brow furrowed, Binnie grabbed a file to put on the Zombie's chair. Madeline was laughing, said "Oh, *you*," as Binnie strolled past them. Capra's hand lingered strangely on Madeline's desk. His eyes flashed.

"Oh, Binnie!" he said. "Before I forget. And then I really have to go. Do you like opera?" Binnie nodded, dumbly. "Are you free this Tuesday? I have two tickets I can't use. For you and a friend. They're excellent seats."

"Sure! Thank you."

He reached into his jacket pocket and handed her an envelope. "There you go. Good night!"

Madeline pulled on her coat. "I'm outta here."

Binnie waved the envelope at her. She'd never actually been to the opera. She'd been inside Lincoln Center once, on a high school trip. The tour guide had said the shallow steps were designed so ladies could descend with ease, the skirts of their gowns trailing behind them. Backstage, they'd seen powdered wigs on wooden heads and bustled costumes, and peered down through a window at the Philharmonic rehearsing. But the red-carpeted stairs and the spangled chandeliers had stuck most vividly in her mind.

Binnie returned to her desk. Beatrice and Rick stared impassively at their computers. When they did this, you could never tell what they were thinking or if they were listening but pretending not to listen. They were experts at the cubicle game.

"As soon as Baxter's gone, we're all cutting out of here early," muttered Beatrice, trained upon her screen. "Oh, and here," she said, finally looking at Binnie and handing her an envelope over the cubicle wall. The plastic window crinkled under her thumb.

Binnie glanced inside at her bonus. One short line and three zeroes. That wasn't nearly enough to fully realize her tower of glass eyes. Maybe if she invested the money? Ha ha! Might as well flush the check down the toilet. Maybe she could pretend she never got the raise and squirrel away the difference. But she had opera tickets and nothing to wear! Well, she thought, trying not to grow too giddy, I have some shopping to do.

❖ ❖ ❖

Binnie took Gary out for dinner at Carmine's.

"So are you still thinking of quitting?" asked Gary. They were already bloated with cheesy garlic bread.

Eating only a few bites of each entree was all that was possible—and painful. They ate out of a profound sense of duty.

"Well," said Binnie, hot pepper buzzing on her lips. "Maybe...maybe I'll stay. At least a little while longer."

"That's what raises are for. To make you say maaaaybe I'll staaaay."

Binnie dabbed the sheen of red oil from her mouth, embarrassed. "I guess."

Saturday morning, they went to Bloomingdale's. Binnie chose a pink satiny sheath, a Nicole Miller body-con, smooth fabric all gathered and crinkly, with short sleeves just off the shoulder. It was on sale but still $300.

"It's really tight," she told the saleswoman, who insisted on a size 2 even though Binnie always wore 4 or 6.

"It's supposed to be," she said. "You've been wearing the wrong size. And anyway the fabric is stretchy if you gain a little weight." To illustrate, the saleswoman tugged at the backside of the dress. "See?"

"I guess I do look good in it," said Binnie, gazing over her shoulder into the mirror. "I always thought of myself as kind of knobby, but lately I'm not."

*Zaftig*, Ruby might joke before patting her bottom.

A bustier and a pair of Spanx smoothed out the body's unsightly little bulges. The saleswoman brought out, also: satiny beige mules, a matching clutch purse, a pashmina shawl, a bloodstone necklace.

"Treat yourself," said the saleswoman with a big-toothed, red-lipped smile.

"I really never do treat myself," said Binnie.

"You look really, really good," said Gary.

Oh well, thought Binnie. What the hell. There goes half the bonus.

At the cash register it began. Or rather, resumed. The self-loathing. *Fuck you*, she thought. *Fuck, fuck, fuck.* She slipped her credit card back into her wallet along with the receipt.

But then: she knew what to do. The rest of the bonus was going to prototypes.

"Your face," Gary said, outside.

"What?"

"It just went through this dramatic—gymnastics."

"Really," she said. She leaned into a kiss, the shopping bag handle cutting into her arm, the plan feeling real.

On Sunday, she said goodbye to Gary and said nothing of getting on the train to Brooklyn right after him to buy at Lowes: a 12 x 24 sheet of clear polycarbonate, a plastic cutter, and a silicone gel gun. She was glad she hadn't discarded her safety goggles and leather gloves when she'd trashed so many other art things.

Tuesday night, after watching a frothy *La Traviata* and tipsy from flutes of champagne, they strolled past the Lincoln Center fountain holding hands, pleasantly dazed by the whirl of colors and music. Binnie pictured Cornell lurking outside the lead soprano's dressing room in hopes of showering her with admiration, then chickening out and slipping a gilded collage under her door: a woman's singing mouth, out of which flew a swallow carrying a limp spray of forget-me-nots. Gary steadied Binnie with a hand at her back as she wobbled, distracted, on her new shoes.

❖ ❖ ❖

A squealing mouse greeted them at Binnie's front door, stuck to the sticky pad by the fridge. Its tiny body shook, its distress high-pitched. "Eww!"

"Want me to take care of it?" Gary asked.

"You don't have to do that for me," Binnie said.

"I like being chivalrous."

"It's okay." She grabbed a plastic grocery bag. In one quick scoop, she enveloped the mouse and the trap, then pushed all the air out of the bag until it stopped squeaking.

"Jesus, Binnie. That's cold."

"Well. It was miserable, so."

With a pinky lifted, she carried the bag to the dumpster outside. If she were another sort of artist, she thought, she would keep the mouse and slice its body lengthwise, preserve the cross-sections of its corpse in formaldehyde and silicone. But that was too dark. And too derivative.

The urgency of the mouse problem had prevented her from quickly clearing her worktable, on which several cut-down pieces of clear polycarbonate sat, waiting to be made into—possibly—the revolving door piece. She still had to play with the "Black Hole" idea. Either way, she needed thin wire for the birds. And, of course, little colorful birds. Taxidermied ones might be going too far, but maybe not?

Gary sat up straight on the futon when she returned, his eyes shining. She couldn't make out what his expression meant. It was neither smiling nor frowning, only a muted wonderment. She didn't want to be so presumptuous as to ask whether he'd glanced at her paltry progress, which she'd failed to hide. Freudian slip?

"What?" she asked. "Did my mercy killing disgust you?"

"I mean. I don't know that I would've used the sticky traps in the first place. But then, mice run rampant in my place. Come here," he said with crinkled brow.

They unfolded the futon and snuggled under the covers. Falling asleep, Gary kissed Binnie's cheek, murmuring, "Good night, sweet killer." She closed her eyes but didn't fall asleep quickly, instead nursing a bruised feeling that spread from her chest up to her face.

❖ ❖ ❖

"Did you enjoy the opera?" Capra asked the next morning by the espresso machine.

"Very much. Thank you. I didn't expect there to be a ballet too. I loved it."

Ballerinas, those gorgeous aliens. No wonder Cornell was smitten. He was otherworldly and so were they.

"I just love the spectacle of opera," Capra said.

She couldn't think of anything smart to say, and from her silence Capra turned away, returned to his office with a shiny red apple. She refilled the faux-ebony box with espresso pods, feeling dumb. Walking back to her desk, she caught Rick glaring in her direction like she'd done something horrible, like she'd strangled his puppy or ruined his life. Was it just because Capra gave her the opera tickets and not him? But soon his eyes slid back to his screen, and she assured herself, as Gary always insisted, that it had nothing to do with her.

Face in a snarl, Capra bounded back toward Binnie.

"Did you order Roman apples?"

Binnie glanced at the lunch chart taped to the wall in her cube.

"It says Gala on the chart," Binnie said.

"And yet this is a Roman apple. Don't order Roman apples in winter. They're mealy."

"Sorry, Mr. Capra. I didn't realize."

"It's all right," he said, voice drawn out, martyr-like. The phone rang. "Pick up."

Binnie pressed mute. "It's Georgina?"

"I'm not here."

He tossed the yellowing apple in the garbage and poured himself another mug of coffee. Baxter clopped into the kitchen, grabbed the coffee carafe before Capra could put it back. The pot slipped to the linoleum, the glass shattering with a loud pop.

"Fuck."

Gingerly, Capra stepped over the mess, sighing as he grumbled to himself, "It's never easy, is it?"

"What did you do?" Zaiman shouted.

Baxter muttered something in reply. Binnie strained to understand. *Boughten? Rotten?*

"What?"

"I said I'll take care of it." Baxter knelt before the mess. Reached for a large, jagged piece the size of a hand.

Binnie jumped in to help, almost tripped and fell into the shards.

"Careful!" Baxter waved her away like she was a gnat.

Madeline said, "Mr. Baxter, leave it." He chucked shards into the garbage. "It should go in paper bags. Leave it. I'll call a janitor."

"It's all right. I'm on it."

"*Leave* it, Bob."

"Shit." He plucked a glass splinter from his palm, wincing.

Rick's hazel eyes gleamed in a way Binnie had never seen them gleam.

# Chapter Six

AT WORK THE FOLLOWING TUESDAY, Binnie eased into Christmas Eve Eve by perusing the headlines. A French investor of aristocratic lineage, Renee-Thierrey de la Villehuchet, had been found dead in his Midtown office. He'd lost an estimated $1.4 billion in the Madoff scandal, a combination of other people's money and his entire life savings. He felt responsible, his brother was quoted as saying, felt he needed to suffer the consequences of his poor decisions. He'd made risky investments and used the earnings to restore the family's ancestral chalet in Brittany. It had once been a point of pride in his life.

Binnie wondered if other, less prominent suicides would occur. People who'd lost everything but whose loss was not as headline-worthy as this. An accountant in Belmore. A high-school economics teacher in Sheepshead Bay. People quietly offing themselves, who might later converge as a single statistic tucked into a footnote.

The kitchen offered refuge from dark thoughts: consolation in a box of jelly donuts, in sugar cookies shaped like dreidels and Christmas trees, in a box of Godiva the size of a Cadillac. She filled a napkin with dark chocolate salted caramels. A sopping sponge sat at the bottom of the kitchen sink, oozing slime.

"You're gonna get some serious cavities," Baxter said, making her jump. She hadn't heard him enter. He reached for a jelly donut. The cut on his palm, unbandaged, had crusted to scarlet. He sank his teeth into the donut, which gushed raspberry goo. Binnie stopped chewing with a bulge of chocolate in her cheek. Pointed to the sticky red splotch at the corner of his sugar-coated mouth. He ran his thumb over it, sucked it clean, winked. Knocked his elbow against hers as he swallowed. Said, in that low voice that seemed to imply conspiracy, "I'm just teasing."

❖ ❖ ❖

In Arlene and Albert's narrow kitchen that night, they formed an assembly line to make latkes for Hanukkah. Arlene shaped the latkes, Binnie manned the frying, Gary plopped them on paper towels, and Albert appraised the process: too thick, too thin, too brown, not brown enough, more oil, too much oil, chop chop, I'm hungry.

After the first dozen, Gary excused himself. Binnie, who'd been surprised he was willing to brave a repeat of Thanksgiving at all, flipped the batch sizzling in the pan, admiring the golden color. When Gary was out of the room, she turned to her mom.

"Hey, so, you guys have, uh, retirement plans, right?"

Arlene leaned on the counter, a half-smile curling. "A pension? Sure. We both do."

"But, like. Do you know how it works? Like, is it invested? In something?"

Arlene looked thoughtful.

Albert said, "Invested, sure."

Arlene nodded.

Binnie said nothing.

"It's solid," Arlene said. Her voice rose into a sing-song. "It's so good to hear you thinking about the *future*, Binnie." Maternal eye sparkle. "*Now* we're talking." In a fit of love, she wrapped Binnie in a hug. "Y'know, now that you have a real job, you ought to start saving. There's that tax credit for first-time homebuyers."

Albert laughed softly, and though he didn't say Binnie ought to partner up with someone financially stable, she could guess where his mind was drifting and bristled.

Gary came back from the bathroom and sidled up to Albert in the doorway, brow furrowed.

"The latkes are burning."

Binnie wriggled out of her mother's arms and chucked the singed cakes onto the oily pile.

"Sour cream!" Albert said, shuffling to the fridge, finger pointing in the air. "Sour cream improves all."

On Christmas Eve, Capra needed a Big Thing Done. An investor in a beer company was suing over a merger. Giddily, he asked Binnie to stay late. "You don't care about Christmas anyway, right?" After the recent bonus and raise, she couldn't complain.

Binnie texted Gary, pushing back their plans to seven. Gary arrived precisely at seven. He waited in the vestibule for half an hour while she kept working.

Downtown, they supped on Shanghai-style soup dumplings. Binnie felt compelled to drink beer, like it would enrich her, now that she had some tiny hand in its production. She thought of doing a piece made up entirely of grasping dolls' hands. Could she somehow animate them, have them actually try to grab things, slowly, creepily? Why did she always come up with impossible ideas, things she had no clue about executing? She guzzled her beer and ordered another. Oh—the grasping hands came from the movie *Labyrinth*. David Bowie of the Goblin King clucked his tongue. Think of something else.

They caught a weird but boring movie at the Film Forum, with lots of long takes focused on ocean waves and little cricks and squeaks that were maybe supposed to evoke sea mammal sounds. Binnie wasn't paying close enough attention to know for sure.

"What'd you think?" Gary asked afterward, as the credits rolled. "No opinion?" Quizzically, he said, "Earth to Binnie?"

She kissed him. "Sorry. None. No opinion."

She still hadn't told him about the brunch thing at the gallery. She didn't want anyone's input on it until she knew what she was doing. If she didn't make a decision soon, she would have to give herself a lobotomy to make do with the path she found herself on, in which economic pressure pushed her into applying for law school.

The omission was starting to feel like lying. If she wanted Gary to come along, she would have to say something soon.

The next day, Christmas, they strolled around Manhattan, resting, as evening fell, on the barricades in an empty Rockefeller Center. She loved Midtown Manhattan on a holiday night, when it was dead quiet and empty.

"You know," said Binnie. "I feel really good around you."

"I do too," said Gary. "Around you." He squeezed her hand. "I love you, Binnie."

Oh! thought Binnie. She wasn't expecting that. She wasn't expecting that at all. Love, so soon? She didn't know what to say or do. She put her arms around him, squeezed and kissed and hugged, and he put his arms around her and squeezed and kissed and hugged right back. She clung to him as if they were the last two humans in an apocalyptic city.

# Chapter Seven

BETWEEN CHRISTMAS and New Year's, an anime porn company wanted to file bankruptcy. Capra said Binnie could take the lead on the paperwork.

"You've shown your diligence at trial. You are perfectly capable of this task."

Sitting in the conference room with Capra and the erstwhile pornographer, a sixty-something white man with a thick mustache, felt only slightly odd. She wished she hadn't sat so her back was turned to the view of the East River. But she was glad she'd worn a suit jacket to the meeting. She felt protected by it.

It was relatively easy to go through the inventory to be liquidated. The cartoonish thumbnail images of the movies were not particularly graphic, though for some reason it was the ones that included "milk" in the title that made her queasy.

On New Year's Eve, a Wednesday, Gary picked Binnie up in the lobby of the Lipstick Building. They strolled, fingers interlocked, down to Curry Hill for dinner. Batting eyelashes at each other in the warm glow of chili-shaped lights, they dipped papadams in sweet chutneys and spicy green and orange sauces, and plotted out an urban hike for Saturday, which promised crisp, cold sunshine. An antique store in West Chelsea sold ornate doorknobs—Victorian, Art Nouveau, Art Deco.

"Door knobs?" He lit up, leaned in. "What are your plans for door knobs?"

Binnie clammed up, wanted to snap, *that's private.* In part because she didn't know. And in part because she thought it was bad luck to share inadequately formed ideas. Spending time with Gary took up a lot of head space, and ideas couldn't all be worked out at the subconscious level. She had to do the painful work of sitting and staring and sitting and arranging, physically searching. Executing. Making that shop the destination was a way to fit her art into their time together, even if she couldn't bring herself to divulge the goal. She didn't want to hurt Gary. She wanted his company, wanted to be with him. Cherished the idea of a long walk. But there was only so much time.

"I'm not sure yet," she said. Crept her hand into to his.

She felt some kinship with Joseph Cornell in this area: his trepidation over romance realized, his suspicion that it might affect his art, ruin his ability to make it. Not that she felt entirely the same. Her feelings didn't stem from the same mixture of Victorian ideals, an imposing mother, and suffocating social anxiety, for one thing. But there was a hook of hesitation in her gut, a desire to have Gary near and yet keep him at arm's length. Providing space for yearning was part of it. She needed to yearn more, she thought. Being hungry sharpened the senses. Making art on a full stomach didn't work well, and maybe being in a happy relationship didn't help much either. Why make art if your love-addled brain chemistry was telling you you had everything you could possibly want?

But that wasn't quite right either.

After dinner, they cozied up on her futon with a sweating bottle of prosecco. The fizz buoyed her up.

"I want to show you something," she said.

Crouching beneath her work table, she opened the garbage bag that hid "Infection," the one piece that was close to done. Inside, the little boy with the ice cream smile shined up at her in the dark. Turmeric dusted the cluster of gluey jujubes that orbited him like a small, yellow moon. Nestled around the boy and the cosmic viral microbe: silk marigolds. Strips of old plaid flannel, similar to what the little boy wore, lined the box. When it was on display, vanilla-scented candles would burn atop the diorama, wax dribbling. Altar-like, the box commemorated a life unknown to her save for a chance encounter on a subway platform. Holding her breath, she lifted it up like it was a baby she'd delivered.

"I think this one is almost done."

Gary joined her. Peered inside.

"This is awesome, Binnie."

"You think?"

"Yes, I think. This is great. What's it called?"

She cleared her throat. "Infection."

"Weird. I love it. Who's the little boy?"

"A stranger. I found the photo on a subway platform."

"You should show Ellen."

"Really?"

"Yes! She's your friend. At an art gallery. And that's like—" he touched her arm excitedly—"that could be your shtick: 'I find old photos on subway platforms and mix it with other cool finds and *boom*: here's my art.'"

"Yeah, but." She knew she shouldn't ask. "Do I really need a shtick? A gimmick?"

"Sure!" He kissed her. "Maybe it isn't that shtick. But you need one. Anyway, we should celebrate." He refilled their glasses. "We'll take it to Ellen! Saturday."

"Saturday."

*Shit or get off the pot* still pierced her sternum and tugged like a fish hook.

"Like you weren't already thinking about it when you were plotting our day in West Chelsea. We'll be near the gallery, right?"

"Saturday. You knew about that?"

"Yes. Ellen invited me. Now put that down and come over here."

❖ ❖ ❖

Binnie couldn't sleep. It was well documented that Cornell liked the company of young women—ballerinas, actresses, college students—and rarely admitted men into his basement studio to see works in progress. He was reluctant to sell his work to dealers but gladly gave collages and dream boxes as gifts to the women he idolized. Relationships, however, never manifested. His painful shyness and obsession with "innocence" prevented that. He'd had his first sexual encounter in his sixties, with an extravagantly exhibitionist performance artist, Yayoi Kusama—this only after he'd gone around asking other artists if they knew any women who'd pose nude. He didn't draw, but he wanted to learn, he said.

Still, that encounter was not a romance. It was a performance, perhaps with Cornell as the audience. Binnie wondered if Kusama snickered at him, amused in the same way Andy Warhol and his tribe were amused by Cornell. (Did Gary find *her* amusing?) They competed among themselves to see whom Cornell would admit into his house and for how long, and how much they'd manage to see. They would pretend to need the bathroom to sneak a peek at the upstairs, at his monk's cell of a bedroom.

❖ ❖ ❖

Filmy yellow light crept through the windows. Binnie wiped slobber from her pillow and expanded into a feline stretch. It was noon. Gary was not in bed. Her head remained on the pillow a moment as she trained a soft gaze on the shaft of sunlight.

Do on New Year's Day what you wish to do the rest of the year.

All that sleep! Time wasted. Pick one thing. One project.

Focus.

Eyes closed, sunlight shining through the pink of her lids, the project came to her: the eyeball tower. A bulbous swirl refracting light.

She smiled.

*Thank you*, she thought.

The toilet flushed. Gary emerged.

"Coffee?"

"All right if I do some work today?"

"You mean work-work?" He frowned.

"Art."

He lit up. Then hesitated. "Oh. You want me to leave?"

"Um, no. No. Of course not. Just, you know, we can chill here for a bit."

Binnie curled up in a ball against the wall and sketched with the notepad against her bare thighs, sheets in a tangle. Eyeballs staring out, eyeballs going googly, eyeballs giving side-eye. Meanwhile, Gary browsed her short stack of books. On Cornell, on dreams. Astronomy. Bird poems. A compendium of famous silent film moons.

He leaned against the wall with the bird book and read for a while. Binnie relaxed into her sketching. Should the eyeballs all glare pointedly in one direction or should they look every which way, or...? The landlady's footsteps crept overhead. A pipe clanked. Gary peered out the window as if looking for a hawk on a rooftop. Cleared his throat.

"How about a bit of fresh air? Before the holiday's over and we have to return to our cubes?"

Binnie uncurled from her hunched position, spine crackling. Quelled a violent wave of frustration. Peeped out the window and squinted while the feeling passed. Snow wobbled in the street, shot through with sunlight. She glanced at the clock; only thirty minutes had passed. Glanced at her notebook.

"Or, I could leave? It's just, you know, one of my few days off."

The flurry did brighten First Avenue's grim-blandness.

"Well. Okay."

She dug out her old upstate boots and they played for the rest of the day, the cold awakening them, all rosy-cheeked plopping in the fluff to make angels. They flung snowballs. Lunched on hot dogs and knishes, dined on pizza and beer. Scents of snow and roasting chestnuts and salted pretzels and the smoke of grilling kebabs melded into a supreme feeling of hominess in the winter city.

◈ ◈ ◈

Ellen's gallery hosted a first Saturday of the year mimosa-infused shindig. A start-your-year-with-art gimmick, full of brightness and hope and boozy bubbles. Outside the gallery, Binnie stalled. "Infection" sat cradled in her hands, wrapped loosely in a kitchen towel. She recalled bringing the lunar terrarium to Professor Lewis's office hours, standing on the threshold, hopeful. The pitiful way her favorite professor had pursed her lips and crooned. Somehow, she'd thought showing her work to an art historian would feel safer than showing it to a working artist. But she'd left feeling dismissed and more clueless than ever. What made her think this would be any better?

Gary, hand on Binnie's back, gently nudged her forward.

A silver-haired man in ankle boots brushed past them, held open the door, and smiled. Faint freckles dotted his face. The man with the youthful features who'd whisked Alexis away at the holiday party. Binnie stumbled in.

Ellen, stationed at the front desk, smiled wide just as Binnie tripped.

"Binnie!"

The covered diorama creaked between them as they hugged.

Ellen began to lift the cloth. Binnie lightly slapped her hand.

The phone rang. Ellen turned her back, answered. Binnie put the box down among the postcards and catalogues, unveiled it. Gary lingered, hopeful. Held her elbow in support.

"Why don't you go look around?" she said.

His mouth curled. "You mean I can't be your manager?" Ellen glanced over her shoulder, held her finger up at them, turned her back again. "I kid," he said. "Holler if you need the hard sell."

He wandered off into the white room, which had been completely transformed since early December. Sinuous wooden sculptures punctured the center of the space. Rusted metal mobiles had been suspended from the ceiling and they twirled, faintly creaking. Enormous encaustics lined one wall, textured squares of indigo, crimson, and gold. Under a set of skylights at the back, a waif in knee-high boots poured drinks. Gary gravitated mimosa-ward.

Ellen kept chattering. She laughed into the phone, glanced over her shoulder at Binnie, laughed again. Standing there exposed, Binnie wanted to shrink into a snail shell. She wanted to cover her snail shell in dirt. She wanted to put the dirt-enrobed shell inside a cedar box. She wanted to sink the box into the bottom of her mind. She folded and unfolded the kitchen towel, considered re-veiling "Infection," leaving.

The lanky silver fox in the ankle boots passed by as Ellen hung up the phone. On his arm hung Alexis in a black sheath dress and high-heeled peep-toe boots. Her toenails cobalt. Ellen glanced at "Infection" and Binnie cringed. Ellen could easily say something before these giants that would change everything. But, in view of the Amazon, her boss, Ellen's mouth stayed shut.

"Now isn't that charming," the Amazon said, her New York body suggesting forward movement even as her head craned back toward Binnie's creation. Her prominent cheeks crabapples. Say something, thought Binnie. Anything. The bit of glue peeping out from the yellow candy didn't, at least, resemble mucus. But standing here before Alexis, she thought the piece leaned too heavily on the power of the photograph.

"We met last month," Binnie blurted. She thought she would vomit on the cobalt toes.

"I remember." The Amazon handed her a card. "Call me."

Binnie's mouth opened but she said nothing. A faint croak issued from her throat; she'd lost all ability to talk. The Amazon wandered out with the man into the brisk day, laughing huskily. What *was* that, she thought she heard him say. Binnie pocketed the card, shrouded the diorama. The excitement that had rendered her temporarily mute flip-flopped to a clammy panic. The laughter wasn't promising. She'd fucked up before she'd even truly begun.

"I gotta go."

Ellen balked. "Wait, what? Why?"

Her eyes strained hot. "Quitting while I'm ahead!"

Gary was looking at a video of a clown-faced naked woman smashing rotten tomatoes onto a kitchen counter with the heel of her hand. Binnie swung the door open and barreled west, toward the High Line. Her plan was to sit in the shadow of the old elevated train tracks on a plastic milk crate with her head between her knees.

Gary soon caught up, stopped her mid-block.

"Why are you running away?"

Mimosa breath coiled in the crystalline air. Across the street, a man swung a garbage bag into a dumpster. An arc of liquid flew in the bag's wake.

"I saw what happened," he said.

"Yeah? I panicked. And she laughed."

"Forget about that. Remember? It isn't always about you?"

"You always say that. Sometimes it *is*!"

"Maybe her friend told her a dirty joke."

"She told me to call. I don't think she was serious."

"She gave you her card. Again! You have to call her. Monday."

Nothing in Alexis's gallery remotely connected to Binnie's work. The place was big and cold. The woman's wardrobe matched the work she chose to display. Clean, bold lines. Even her bone structure matched. Binnie felt like a Disney mouse, pink paws joined prayerfully at a giant. *Don't crush me.* Please.

She kept walking toward the Hudson. Gary followed. He put his arm around her. She tilted her head onto his shoulder and sniffled.

"I'm concerned about you," he murmured.

Crushing a spirit is easier than crushing a mouse; it doesn't bleed.

# Chapter Eight

"**H**AIL TO the conquering yadda yadda," Zaiman said to Capra after New Year's, with a little two-fingered salute.

"One day of work for twenty grand ain't bad, right?" Capra had won the beer thing. Where was Binnie's cut? An extra thirty bucks for the ninety minutes she'd stayed late, while he got twenty grand? Blarg.

She swilled the espresso she'd made from an emerald pod. *Essence of soylent green,* she joked bitterly with herself. Someone somewhere had died for her coffee, surely. Meanwhile, Capra was planning to take Margaret out for a celebratory dinner at their favorite Michelin-starred restaurant—in San Sebastian.

"Binnie," said Zaiman, "would you scan this and email it to me?"

His 2007 tax return. He'd made $2 million. He always said his teeth were bad because when he was growing up his parents never had money for the dentist; he was a true by-your-own-boots-strapper. (Thanks to free college in the sixties.)

Binnie collated documents in the quiet of the conference room. Thick gray clouds replaced the weekend's stark sunshine. They hovered low over Queens in a stone dome. Threatened sleet rather than snow. But the cold wet outside promised release from the Lipstick Building's dry recycled air, which she now suspected of causing her migraines, possibly of slowly killing her.

At lunch, Binnie huddled beneath the building's granite columns and gulped damp January wind. The sleet fell in sharp drops against her cheeks. She spied Baxter partially hidden by another column, staring at 53rd street, cigarette smoke coiling from his fingers. A sinking feeling pushed her back into the marbled lobby. Upstairs, she slipped into the empty office that had been Paul's. She pretended he hadn't been laid off but had left to pursue creative projects, was now filming on location in Prague or Saigon. Or maybe, despite being laid off, he'd decided to throw caution to the wind, do just that. Goosepimpled from the cold, trembling, she called Alexis Thorne. It went straight to voicemail.

"This is Alexis. Leave a message." The curator's low voice, quick and forthright.

Binnie forced herself not to hang up.

"Himyname'sBinnieGreenson," she said, legs shaking. Slowed down. "I came to the gallery on Saturday. I had the diorama with the picture of the boy and the marigolds. You said to call." She hung up. Dialed again, sweating. Left her number. Doofus. Stared at the phone, willing the little red light to glow with Alexis's call.

At the espresso machine she brewed one of the gold pods. An empty box of chocolates sat ravaged in the trash. Someone had eaten them all overnight. Out from behind the trash can, a shiny black roach scuttled. Its bloated body made its gait wobbly.

"Eeeeegh!"

"What?" asked Beatrice from the doorway. Binnie pointed. Beatrice yipped a high-pitched squeal that Binnie never would've expected could come from her contralto voice box. The Zombie ambled out of his office, chewing gum and hitching up his belt.

"What's the problem, ladies?" They pointed at the roach, which now lingered fearlessly on the white linoleum. "Oh, no. I'm not killing that thing." He took an empty tissue box out of the trash, bent uneasily, and turned it over on top of the bug.

"Now what?"

Rick burst in with a can of Raid. "Everyone get out," he said. He shielded his mouth and nose with the crook of his arm, lifted the tissue box and sprayed and sprayed underneath it as the bug danced in its poison shower, then scurried under a cabinet and disappeared, presumably to die alone.

"Let me know if you see any more roaches," said Beatrice. Binnie shuddered. A fancy building like the Lipstick should not have pests, she muttered. "You know, the building has a new management company, and they took pest control out of the standard package. Everyone has to pay extra."

"Ugh."

"One bad tenant can ruin a whole building."

❖ ❖ ❖

Binnie regretted spending so much of her bonus on non-art things. *Feed the art, you dumbass,* she thought as she left work that day. She wandered down 53rd Street, west to the MoMA. Joseph Beuys, Sol LeWitt, Jean Prouvé, Batiste Madalena. She wound her way through each special exhibit, cramming images into her brain. Some of Beuys's small sculptures, inside vitrines, were delicate like Cornell's assemblages. But his belief that art had to connect with society, documented in a blurb about his political life, felt to Binnie like a reproach, like he had pointed at her feeling of inarticulation and left a bruise. Sol LeWitt's large wall drawings, faint white lines on black, both straight and not, continuous and broken, made her skin itch. The focus on mass production in Jean Prouvé's design atelier felt like something she was supposed to nod at with appreciation but it mostly annoyed her. Maybe that was what annoyed her about silicone: the idea that she could make a mold of anything and repeat it over and over. It was a cool technique, but also, like...maybe try making something one-of-a-kind and special? Whatever that meant.

Madalena's hand-painted film posters from the 1920s, at least, had a little something-something. "The

Freshman" reminded Binnie of F. Scott Fitzgerald's lesser fiction, yet appeared soaked in so much raspberry and grape Kool-Aid you could drink from it. Greta Garbo as "The Mysterious Lady" pulled Binnie across the room with intense, heavy-lidded eyes; next to her, a too-kooky woman with Medusa curls and a dollar bill on her cheek gaped out from "The Beggar on Horseback" poster. In a third piece, a femme fatale Binnie had never heard of, Pola Negri of "Hotel Imperial," performed the most intense over-the shoulder side-eye Binnie had ever seen.

Not a single one of the special exhibits focused on stuff made by a woman. Was that her problem? The lack of role models? There were things mixed here and there in the permanent collections, of course. As if she hadn't spent enough on the admission ticket, she found herself in the museum store purchasing a hot-pink book: *Infinity Net*, the autobiography of Yayoi Kusama, the artist she was sure she would loathe for her unkindness to Joseph Cornell.

At home, she flipped through the book. When she was a girl, Kusama wrote, a field of violets sang to her.

Binnie kept the book open to that page, put her pillow on top, and went to sleep hoping for a miracle.

❖ ❖ ❖

Each day that Alexis did not call Binnie back, she died a little inside. She didn't want to say anything to Ellen; she wasn't sure a nudge from Ellen would do any good.

You had to be really good to be pushy, was the thing. She twisted up in knots, resentful of Ellen and Gary for making her do this too early.

But then, but then. What was she to do with the overpriced rat-hole she lived in now? She'd cut the cord so as not to become a stone baby in Ruby's t(w)omb. But she was more beholden than ever to her stupid job, where she took pitiful solace in being called "perfectly capable," pitiful solace in doing something "important" like help-ing a porno company go out of business.

This private torment was easy to hide. She'd done it all through the trial and been praised for her calm demeanor. But that didn't mean it ever went away.

❖ ❖ ❖

Inauguration Day reinvigorated the office's spirit, brought back the optimistic cheer of Election Day. The partners gathered around Capra's computer to watch news cover-age of the parade, while the Zombie, Beatrice, and Binnie gathered around Madeline's computer. The Obamas, their breath curling in the winter air, marched down the frigid streets of Washington, asphalt sparkling with hoarfrost, Michelle in a dreamy gold power dress, everyone smiling, smiling, smiling.

The only person in the office who did not beam was Rick. His computer wallpaper still showed Eliot Spitzer's contrite face after his rocketing career was dashed by scandal. *What a douche*, he'd once said to Binnie of the former governor.

"Our little reactionary," Zaiman joked that morning, slapping Rick on the back. "Mmhm," said Beatrice. "Oh, be nice," said Madeline, jovial.

Binnie smiled. Rick sneered. He sat by himself in his cubicle and muttered something about opening a Twitter account. When Obama's address began, Madeline turned up the volume. The Zombie leaned in, smelling of cigarettes and Doublemint gum.

The words were rousing, Binnie thought, if a tad cerebral. "Homes have been lost; jobs shed; businesses shuttered. Our health care is too costly; our schools fail too many; and each day brings further evidence that the ways we use energy strengthen our adversaries and threaten our planet. These are the indicators of crisis, subject to data and statistics. Less measurable but no less profound is a sapping of confidence across our land, a nagging fear that America's decline is inevitable..."

Alone in his cubicle in the center of the office, Rick snorted with laughter. The Zombie's face crinkled in disdain. Binnie peeked around the reception wall at the partners: Zaiman hunched over Capra in his chair, Baxter's arms crossed and elbows cradled. Were the words getting through? On the face of it, they cared deeply about the law. Their expressions displayed appropriate reverence for a historic moment. But would anything change?

"We remain a young Nation, but in the words of Scripture, the time has come to set aside childish things."

Change. The desire was in Binnie's fingertips, the meaning of it not yet there, only the yearning, but maybe that was okay. First you have to *want*.

❖ ❖ ❖

The holiday gift baskets ceased. Binnie was grateful. Perhaps the cessation of gorging would help her think. Beatrice went on her quarterly cleanse diet, eating nothing but greens and drinking nothing but water with a half lemon floating in the glass, proclaiming sugar as poison. Madeline joined the pact to eliminate sugar from her diet. Beatrice once again printed out the regimen and gave it to Binnie, and Binnie once again put it in her purse to throw out later.

Industrial-size roaches kept appearing; the Zombie kept saying he would not kill them. (Binnie never would have pegged him as an animal lover.) The killing was left to Rick and sometimes Capra.

In Binnie's daily perusal of Madoff developments, she found another suicide. This article was shorter, the deceased investor being of less impressive provenance but still worthy of note. A retired British military officer who'd lost his life savings and shot himself in the head. There were human-interest stories, too, accompanied by pictures of frail elderly people leaning on walkers. Elderly people who'd planned retirements in expensive assisted-living communities, thinking their investment in Madoff's fund would carry them comfortably to the end of their days.

"Look at these people, Dick," she said to the Zombie, when he came at her with a stack of files.

"Yeah." He sounded weary.

"That'll be me one day."

"What do you mean?"

"Student loans. I'm in the hole like them. I'll work until I die."

"Binnie, Binnie, Binnie. I'm $80,000 in the hole. Don't worry. We'll *all* be working till we die." What he didn't say, and what Binnie wondered, was whether he thought he'd make partner one day so the point would become moot. Though that wouldn't—couldn't—happen for everyone. He'd have to leave CZB, go someplace where the grind was more punishing. Would other law firms have the same implicit visual standards for making partner? He tossed the files flagged with a hundred Post-it notes on her desk. Deadpan, he said, "Capra needs this by four."

"Thanks, Dick."

"Uh huh," he said. "You bet."

She googled "Madoff" and "suicide" to see if anyone else had done themselves in, but only the two stories of the Frenchman and the Brit appeared.

That Sunday, after seeing Gary off to the subway, Binnie headed south on First Avenue, trying to stay connected with that feeling she'd gotten in her fingertips, the feeling that she must *do*. Scrounge for materials, find stuff to light a spark. All the way down in Alphabet City, she stumbled on a curiosity shop, found three taxidermied sparrows. They weren't the flamboyant kind of bird she'd envisioned for the revolving door and "Black Hole" piece(s), but they were the right size for now. She cupped them in her palms.

"How old are these?" she asked the shopkeep, a

sturdy, ruddy-cheeked woman who sat with her hands on her knees, poised to tell a story.

"How old do you want them to be?" She had an oracle quality about her, this woman. A cash-only oracle. Binnie withdrew $80 from the store's ATM and bought the sparrows.

The sun was setting as she arrived home, having found no discarded treasures along the sidewalks. *Ugh, don't scrounge in the garbage*, she kept hearing Arlene say. (It was an old habit.)

Inside, she rested the birds on her worktable and got the kettle going. It was only after she defrosted herself with a cup of tea that the panic reemerged. With trepidation, she sat at the table. Managed to pause the spiral of panic before she touched the sparrows again, the most delicate tap of fingertips to feathers. Compared to the pieces of clear polycarbonate she'd set aside for the revolving door, the birds would be outsized. Maybe that would be good? Maybe she needed bigger birds, smaller people.

❖ ❖ ❖

One morning at the end of January, Binnie considered saying something to Ellen about Alexis. Would Ellen say *just call her again, dummy*? Or would she say *let it go, it's clear she's not interested*? She couldn't stand the contrast between the obviousness and clarity of Ellen's point of view and the opaque muck of her own. *Clear as mud*, her father liked to say. She fidgeted her mouse to wake up her computer from its slumber, then shuffled to the kitchen and poured herself black coffee, spilling dark driblets on the counter. Back at her desk, after rummaging through her email and minimizing Outlook, a handful of unfamiliar PDFs on the desktop caught her eye. She hadn't scanned anything recently, never saved things to her desktop, and always gave files meaningful names. These had names generated by the scanner, just the date with no dashes, a run-on string of numbers.

Someone had been using her computer. Since last night?

She opened one PDF and her throat constricted: there on her desktop was a huge, full-color, high-resolution image of Georgina, topless, in a g-string, holding two exquisitely frosted pastel pink cupcakes in front of her chest, with just enough side boob displaying the perkiness of her breasts.

Binnie closed the file—her whole being, she was sure, transformed red. She glanced around to see if anyone had seen. Madeline was behind the reception wall on the phone, having one of her long murmuring conversations with a friend or relative. Beatrice appeared lost in a spreadsheet. Rick had some complicated excavation project going in the file room. Zaiman reclined in his chair, browsing the *New York Law Journal*. Capra was taking a lengthy conference call behind closed doors. The Zombie was leaving the kitchen with his hourly dose of caffeine, taking the long way around the oval of the Lipstick back toward his office.

Quickly, she opened and closed each PDF, all photos of a topless and g-stringed Georgina: splayed belly-down on a bed; licking vanilla frosting off a cupcake; lying on her back with "I love you, Bernie" written in baby-blue icing on her belly while she arched her eyebrow into a come-hither stare, pink frosting (buttercream?) hiding her nipples. Why were these on her computer?

Why now? Why her? Why this? Should she delete them? Hide them in a file in Capra's S:/ drive folder? Her ice-block hands cooled her hot cheeks, hopefully draining the beet-redness of them.

Rick came out of the file room with a pile of expandable files and plunked them on his desk.

"Morning," she said to him, probing for a clue.

"Morning," he said, voice gelid and eyelids lowered to a nonchalant deadness.

Binnie browsed her computer in search of clues. The offending PDFs not only sat on her desktop, they had been emailed *from* Binnie's work email *to* an email she'd never seen before, HoneyBear6969@gmail.com. Now she was both panicked and angry. What kind of trail was someone trying to leave? And who was HoneyBear6969@ gmail.com? A porn site? She didn't recognize it from the Chapter 7 bankruptcy case. The photos were more boudoir than porn, she had to admit. But. Still. This was very bad. She could not, of course, google this email address here. She'd do it as soon as she got home.

She created a nest of file folders three layers deep inside an already existing "Stuff for Capra" folder inside the "Paralegal" folder (which held a gym membership confirmation, a certificate attesting to the authenticity of a piece of art he'd bought, a tax return) and moved all the PDFs there under **S:/Paralegal/Stuff_for_Capra/Misc/Feb2009/G**. Perhaps the "G" would be taken for a folder mistakenly created and abandoned. In any case, no one ever looked inside the Paralegal folder. In the collage by Binnie's computer, Tamara Toumanova's hands seemed less exalted, more fatalistic: the whole gesture an elegant shrug.

Maybe Capra had scanned the images early that morning, didn't want them on his own computer. But that made little sense. Was it possible someone had swiped the images from his office, scanned them for their own private use? Zaiman? Dick? Again, why would that person be so careless? None of the men in the office were dumb. Were they? It seemed someone wanted Binnie to see the images.

"Tea time," Madeline exclaimed somewhat softly as she came around the corner. She paused at Binnie's desk. "You look pale! Are you okay?"

"I feel a little sick to my stomach, come to think of it."

"No, you really do look pale." Madeline touched her forehead in search of a fever. She disappeared into the kitchen and brought back an icepack wrapped in a paper towel. "Put this on your forehead."

"O-kay."

"Want some lavender tea?"

"O-kay."

It was nice of Madeline to take care of her. It was nice to have someone maternal in the office.

Why were her eyes leaking?

Madeline brought the tea out in a paper cup (she never used the firm-branded mugs, which others left in the sink for "someone"—her—to wash at the end of each day) and Binnie drank it boiling hot until she felt the heat go into her fingers and toes.

"Thank you," Binnie said a little later, standing over Madeline at her desk. "I do feel better." Madeline tore herself from a photo stream of 100 Unbelievable UFO Sightings. A silver, blurred disc in a New Mexico night sky.

"You're quite welcome," Madeline said brusquely.

# Chapter Nine

ONE THURSDAY MORNING in February, Binnie came in early to cover for Madeline, who was visiting her parents in Guyana. The office would be quiet; all she had to do was answer the occasional call and transfer it to voicemail. With the lights still off, she dumped her stuff at her desk, rubbing her sleepy eyes, and ambled toward the kitchen to brew the coffee. The room appeared darker than usual, despite the fact that it was windowless, as if someone the night before had shut off all the machinery sporting glowing buttons.

Then the darkness—somehow—squirmed.

My eyes must be wonky, she thought for a split second. Maybe she'd rubbed them too vigorously? She flipped the light switch and her finger brushed something smooth and hard that darted away. Hundreds, maybe thousands, of shining roaches scuttled away from the harsh fluorescent light, their collective tiny feet a subtle *tic-a-tic-a-tic-a*. Binnie grabbed her bag and ran outside screaming;

after she dry-heaved by the elevator, she called Beatrice, who let out a long, disgusted moan.

Capra finally agreed to hire an exterminator, and Binnie wondered if CZB had been the "bad tenant" all along, not opting into the extra charge for pest control. No one could work remotely, away from the roaches— they had to be able to answer the phones, access the files. No, it wouldn't do to let the roaches keep them away from work. Baxter jumped in, offering to find a pest control company. He was waiting on news of the PanCorp appeal. Zaiman had been taunting him about his no-good loser clients who didn't pay, and he needed something proactive to do. (He didn't say all this in so many words, but Binnie filled in the blanks.)

Were they the breed of roach that ate the insides of televisions, Binnie wondered? Munching the guts of the office's humming servers. She perched at the edge of her seat all day, as if she might crunch against a teeming coven of roaches on the back of her chair, as if they might slip into her pants pockets and infest her studio, as if they might fall from the drop ceiling into her shirt collar, making her dance convulsively.

❖ ❖ ❖

The next day, Friday, Madeline was still out. Binnie arrived early again. The office was empty and quiet. Roaches hate humans, Binnie had heard once, as she braced herself to switch on the lights. They need our food, but they hate our smell. To save herself from disgust, to allow any roaches lingering in the dark to scuttle quickly from the light, she closed her eyes and kept them shut for five seconds after hitting the switch, stomping her feet to avoid any chance of hearing their movement. Eyes open, no horde. She breathed.

The coffee pot burbled. Binnie crouched before the fridge, filling it with dozens of tiny water bottles. She rose, light-headed. The fridge door slammed shut.

A figure passed in the hall, as if from nowhere— Binnie's heart jumped and she half-shouted.

"Aw, did I scare you?" Baxter leaned back into the doorway. He wasn't wearing shoes, had been creeping around like a ninja.

"You did."

"Sorry, Bin. Mind if I call you Bin?"

"Like a trash bin?"

"Nah..." He smiled and swiped his hand in the air. "Like a, like a, oh, you know. Bin. Bin." His hand waved about in search of words. "It sounds cute." With just the two of them in the office, his tone took on a dollop-smidge too much flirtatiousness.

"Uh huh."

The phone rang, a relief.

"It's Harrison."

Baxter grimaced, face darkening. He disappeared around the bend and hollered, "Send him through!" His thick post-trial voice of defeat bled through the command, in anticipation of dealing with PanCorp. Had he slept in the office or simply arrived at an ungodly hour? Why had he been working in the dark?

❖ ❖ ❖

A white bakery box arrived mid-morning: a gift from a client of Baxter's from New Orleans. Binnie delivered it to Baxter, who was leaning toward his computer with a twisted mouth, as if his glasses no longer worked. A heavenly aroma wafted from the box despite it being closed, a familiar mélange she couldn't quite parse. The heft of it suggested, perhaps, several sticks of butter.

"For me?"

"From Verdier."

Baxter leaned back in his chair, burgundy tie slightly askew. "No way. That old dog." Zaiman had called him a criminal, but Zaiman said that about half of Baxter's clients. Capra disliked Verdier too. But Baxter had leads on other clients. Gulf coast oil. He needed a second OilCo-type case to make good on the PanCorp losses. And Binnie wondered, still, about possible Madoff losses. "Set it down over there."

Binnie balanced the box atop a pile of scrap paper blackened with thousands of inky hatch-mark doodles. The neatness of his desk during her year-end review was long gone.

❖ ❖ ❖

Baxter left early that day. He was feeling under the weather, he said. Before he left, he asked Binnie to serve an eighty-page brief to twelve people. She was glad he went home sick before she photocopied and bound everything, so he couldn't change his mind and make her rip out twelve spines and trash a thousand sheets of paper and crank through the copier another thousand.

Maybe he won't come back, she thought.

You're evil, she thought.

The white box remained on his credenza next to an assortment of pain relievers and vitamin supplements. Pepto Bismol. B-Stress Complex. Kava kava. Extended-release potassium. She picked up the potassium and read its benefits: "Potassium is embedded in the entire process of thought moving through the brain, commanding muscles to move—"

"If you really want to murder someone," her sixth grade Life Science teacher had once said, "give them an extremely high dose of potassium. Potassium naturally increases in the body upon death, and so, you see, it's a lethal agent impossible to detect." The kids used to mock him for the chalk dust always on the crotch of his black pants, which came from adjusting his balls when his back was to the class, as if tweens didn't track such transgressions. She still remembered the Needs Improvement he'd given her report on oysters, about how sand would irritate their stomachs and out came the pearls.

Was this place enough of an irritant to make her emit pearls?

She imagined Zaiman chastising Baxter about the mess, about leaving such personal things out in the open; perhaps he'd been in search of a remedy before giving up and going home. *Stop snooping.* Binnie wanted to tear open the cake box and devour whatever was inside. She opened the lid a crack for a peek. Green and yellow sprinkles gleamed. A whiff of yeasty cake—butter, cinnamon, vanilla. She lowered her nose to it. Lemon zest. That last scent shot happiness to her brain. How had she never considered grating lemon peel to enhance her mood?

During the holidays, she'd grown accustomed to the endless stream of treats, the hourly highs. Now, in the new year, Beatrice and Madeline were cleansing themselves of sugar and other licit drugs. But Binnie, leaving the cake on the credenza, found herself in the kitchen making a double espresso and dumping several packets of sugar in the little cup.

As she stirred, she thought about her glass-eye tower and her doll-hand idea, the revolving door and the black hole in the rooftop with birds flying above it. Thought about the empty Madoff offices downstairs, the two suicides, the news of more layoffs in the larger firms, including Latham & Watkins, the huge one downstairs. About how, the night Gary said I love you, she'd thought of an empty Rockefeller Center as apocalyptic.

She downed the espresso, harsh and sweet.

A man in a blue jump suit and blue cap appeared in the kitchen with a dirty metal tank of something strapped to his back.

"Hello dear," he said. Wrinkles around his eyes and mouth swarmed into a gold-toothed smile. His eyes sparkled warmth, like an all-knowing fairy godfather. A long metal wand snaked out of the tank. He lifted it and said, with quiet pride, "Pest control." He knew he was here to save the day.

"Oh," said Binnie, her brain still halfway stuck in her dreamy apocalypse. "You'll have to talk to Beatrice, over there," she said, pointing at the cubicle.

"Already did," he said. "Just need you to clear out so I can spray this room." Why did she find him so enigmatic? His eyes and smile beamed from another time, another life. "All the food is well-sealed?" The narrow room was empty but for office supplies and dirty coffee cups in the sink; she nodded, still feeling spacey. To his "All right then," she wandered out of the kitchen and settled at her desk. A spraying sound came through the closed door. Liquid poison.

"Quite reasonably priced," she heard Beatrice say to Madeline behind the reception wall. "Baxter found them."

Eyes unfocused, Binnie imagined the whole building empty, like the empty buildings of downtown Wilmington, only a hundred times bigger and more catastrophic. What if the whole building—echoing, abandoned—became an art squat?

The light would be different, of course. Not the harsh white flickering she'd become accustomed to but the sun, fractured by the surrounding skyscrapers, the relentless curve of the Lipstick Building's stacked ovals. What would the thing be, abandoned and given over to art? How many walls could be knocked down without the structure collapsing? And how many panthers could she set loose, and what would it look like from across the street, watching them dart by the windows, sleek and black-furred and hungry? Knocking over potted plants, heaps of black soil spilling from cracked terracotta as they lunged at the throats of hedge fund managers.

Perhaps in the basement mail room, a vast set of show-bright light bulbs, the kind that lined vanity mirrors in green rooms. Walls lined with them, to light the dark. To make the viewer squint.

There would be a level replicating the experience of a migraine—floating lights, a slight hint of green on the walls, a bare floor scattered with dust and grit, and an enormous rusted pipe slowly rotating through one side of the space. Slowly expanding and contracting, creaking as it went.

There would be a floor dedicated to office supply hazards—stacks of papers, slippery linoleum, piles of glinting thumb tacks, errant staple guns shooting overhead. Walls lined with rusting paper cutters, their blades yawning open, apt to crash down any minute in a pile of corroded metal promising tetanus.

Was this all derivative? Very well then, it shall be derivative.

One floor would be frozen—she'd set the thermostat impossibly low and spray the place with liquid nitrogen. Icicles forming in ceiling grates. Was it the rings of hell she was constructing? Should there be a man in that ring, eternally munching on his colleague's brain?

The hot floor would contain vats of steaming black coffee, a bitter stink of burnt grounds and toner fumes. Wallpapering this floor would be documents from tobacco companies, dizzying red text printed on pink paper. Perhaps here we'd have moaning figures, neckties draped over their shoulders, parched mouths panting at the vats of coffee, unable to drink.

Bright white walls and bright white floors would comprise the penultimate level. Feathers, glitter, and marshmallow fluff would drip down the walls, with— why not?—projections of hardcore pornography. Or the porn could be projected onto piles of white feathers scattered on the ground, with a looping soundtrack of smacks and squishes.

On the rooftop, the crown jewel: an enormous diamond-encrusted Buddha, his belly cut open so you could enter it. Warm and red inside, a mix of ruby rhinestones and winking LEDs and square packets of deep-red liquid. The greatest surprise being the portal inside of the belly swallowing you up, never to return.

❖ ❖ ❖

An aura of wonder and triumph buzzed behind Binnie's eyes. How in the hell would she ever get the chance to make such an installation? She wanted to go back into that world again and again. What else would she see?

The exterminator emerged from the kitchen, closed the door behind him.

"You all best clear out now," he told Beatrice. "I'm going to spray the rest of the office. Stuff's tasteless and odorless, so don't go thinking it's not there. It is. But it'll be safe again by Monday."

Beatrice went around the office informing everyone they had to leave immediately. Madeline reminded

Beatrice of that summer five years ago when the whole city had lost power and one associate got left behind, working on his laptop in the dark; everyone had climbed down thirty-four flights of stairs together except this one schmo who had to find his way all by himself.

During the blackout of 2003, Binnie and Gary had been at the terrible internship where they first became friends. The CD company, which was in SoHo, sent everyone home. Binnie and Gary strolled over the Brooklyn Bridge, giddy. A kind of summer snow day. Bars beckoned throngs of people into cool dark rooms for free beer, eager to have it drunk before it spoiled. Neither of them wanted to return to their un-air-conditioned homes. So they drank a few pints, then tipsily rescued melting ice cream sandwiches from a bodega, walking on together all the way to Binnie's parents' place. Binnie had wanted to kiss him then, but she had her Banksy wannabe squatting in a barn outside Poughkeepsie and he was seeing a girl in Montclair, New Jersey. So the mensch went off by himself, head tilted into the night, to his rented room in Sunset Park.

The exterminator sprayed the copy room, the file room, and each emptied office. He came into the clerical area with a gentle, bemused smile. This was what he did all day, Binnie thought, pulling on her coat. Kill things. How was he so calm, so sweet? *Pest control saves the day.*

Faintly, in her mind's ear, a panther growled.

❖ ❖ ❖

Slouching home, Binnie cultivated that triumphant buzz. Tried to focus on her vision for the installation without getting hit by a bus. In the studio she immediately parked herself at her work table and sketched a cross-section of the Lipstick Building. Matthew Barney's Cremaster Cycle came to mind, the goat man tap dancing in the white swirl of the Guggenheim. This could not be that. Not some high-production film to watch at a remove. She wanted to walk *inside* of it, feel the dusty gray carpet under her feet. Smell the panther droppings, the vats of burnt coffee and toner fluid. Let the summer sun beat down on her skin through the windows. Let the too-cold floor give goosebumps, runny noses, hard nipples, shrunken balls. Fingers could run through the piles and piles of white feathers, faintly sparkling on contact with the glitter and sticky with the marshmallow fluff. The porno floor should smell subtly of sex.

Good, she thought. This was good.

The waistband of her pants chafed her belly, the button ready to pop off. She shot up from the seat and peeled off her work clothes, finding a red line circling her torso. In a sweatsuit, she plopped back down in her hard wooden seat. She wasn't actually all that great at drawing—one of the reasons she'd been attracted to Cornell's work, at first. But she sketched and noted. And sketched. And sketched.

Gary called at seven. Her phone was set to vibrate, so she hadn't noticed his three previous texts. But somehow, now, she noticed his call. The pulsing red glow of her flip phone. Whereas before that glow had conveyed Gary's affection, now it conveyed irritation.

"I thought we were meeting in Union Square," he said.

Binnie slapped her forehead and blushed. "Jesus. I'm so sorry," she said. "I'll get there as soon as I can." She threw on jeans and a sweater, tumbled down the stairs and out the door, and, at a bodega on the way, plucked from a plastic tub the biggest, manliest sunflower.

"I'm really sorry," she said again, when they met across the street from the Virgin Megastore. Steam puffed out of the hole in the public art piece next door. Maybe steam could be on her hot floor? Vats of boiling water? Tea kettles whistling alarm? She fixed her attention back on Gary, handing him the sunflower. Over his shoulder, the other monumental piece of public art flickered onward: a giant electronic clock, time rushing away from her.

"It's all right," he said, clearly still annoyed.

She nestled her face into his shoulder. He took the flower and gently tapped her cheek with it. "Boop," he said. The gesture didn't feel right, and in her fragile state she could tell it didn't feel right to him either, but they kissed, somewhat chastely. Tucking her arm into his, she squeezed him to her side as they strolled, hips bumping. Time was rushing away but it would also wash away this not-right feeling, she thought. When everything came into balance.

❖ ❖ ❖

They settled on a movie, *Synechdoche, New York*, about an ambitious playwright who wins a MacArthur Genius grant and attempts to put on a play by making a replica of New York City inside a warehouse. The playwright's first wife is a miniature portraitist who separates from him as her career explodes. Binnie gnawed on her finger-nails throughout the movie. The idea of a city within a warehouse made her mind reel. The trance-like strange-ness of the movie amplified the dreaminess she sought in her dioramas, as if her skull had cracked open and her creative juices had mixed with an invasive thickening agent. It would be difficult to scoop her ideas back in and solder shut the opening.

They sat in the empty theater as the credits scrolled. Gary stood, held out his hand.

"I need a glass of wine," she said. He helped her up.

At the ebony bar of a tapas restaurant, they huddled close, nibbling on blanched asparagus, fried octopus, potato and ham croquettes. They shared a bottle of Malbec. Gary insisted on paying, so Binnie had ordered less than she wanted. But Gary ordered more, and like a good grandmother, encouraged her to eat.

"You'll never turn into a pink flamingo if you don't eat this shrimp," he said, pushing toward her a dish of them sizzling in garlic oil.

"Gary. How did you know my heart-of-hearts desire to be a flamingo?"

"I've known you for years. And I've seen the bird books on your shelf. I know two and two is five." Binnie took a big gulp of wine, pictured her teeth absorbing its purple tint. "Did you ever call that curator?"

She winced. "Yeah. She never called back."

"Oh, well. It was worth a shot." He put the last croquette on her plate. Sullenly, she let its crisp shell collapse in her mouth, salty potato puree burning her tongue. His reaction was underwhelming. So quick to accept defeat? "You'll try someone else," he offered. "Or call her back. Better yet, both." The backpedaling was nice, she supposed. She nodded to placate him. Excused herself.

"Hey," he said when she returned from the ladies' room. "You've inspired me." On a cocktail napkin he'd drawn a cartoon female figure, hair faintly resembling Binnie's mad-scientist wispy curls frizzing out from a bun. The figure held, in a Mickey-Mouse hand, a cluster not unlike the jujubes of "Infection". "I'm your first follower. The school of Binnie!"

Binnie stood next to him on the high stool and slid her arm around his warm waist. "Oh, dear acolyte. " She pressed her cheek to his and squeezed. "Are those stink lines coming out of my head?"

"Genius radio waves." He palmed the tips of her frizz and closed his eyes as if absorbing radiant energy.

# Chapter Ten

IF IT IS POSSIBLE for a Monday morning to be sweetly sleepy, Binnie found that Monday in February to be so. Cars honking, dogs barking, cabbies yelling—it all softened into a haze. Perhaps it was the approach of a Valentine's Day that she actually cared to celebrate; she planned to fashion for Gary a jewel-like heart made of red gummy worms.

The soft haze followed Binnie into the Lipstick Building. Madeline greeted her warmly, peaceful and refreshed from her vacation. And the approach of Mardi Gras, a holiday Binnie didn't celebrate, presented an opportunity to click through photo streams of sequined and feathered carnival masks and muted videos of massive samba numbers.

Then the phones rang, multiple calls at once, and Madeline and Binnie and Beatrice and Rick all answered in rapid succession, and then Capra was in the hall, face the color of chili peppers, yelling about a mistake in the brief served to a dozen people on Friday afternoon. Binnie couldn't explain what had happened, she'd have to figure it out, and in the meantime the phone rang again and Capra was in his office and she was in the kitchen, where Friday's dirty cups were gone, presumably scrubbed by Madeline. A new batch was sure to come. Binnie found a freshly opened bag of coffee and made a pot—temporary salvation!—she felt that her face had already turned upside down and inside out, and puckered, and was trying to scurry into her skull.

Her ears burned, anticipating the further wrath of Capra. She resolved not to hide in the kitchen. She prepared a cup of coffee for him the way he drank it: no cream, no sugar. No brown drips marred the white mug or the black, sans-serif Capra, Zaiman, Baxter LLP logo. She thudded down the carpeted hall toward his office.

Baxter barreled toward her at a right angle, toward Capra's doorway, open white cake box in hand. A square of paper fluttered from the box to the carpet.

"What's always coming but never comes?" Baxter said loudly, buoyantly, outside Capra's office—oblivious to the remnants of furor, or maybe trying to diffuse them. Binnie picked up the greasy bit of paper.

Capra slammed his phone in the receiver. "I don't know, Bob, what?"

"Your wife," Rick muttered. Beatrice sucked her tongue.

*Which wife*, Binnie stopped herself from asking.

"Tomorrow," bellowed Baxter.

"And any decision Bob Baxter makes," Capra snapped. *Ba-dum-ching.* He bared his teeth.

Baxter smiled before Capra could recant and opine on his *bad* decisions. "Morning, Binnie," Baxter said, punchily. He ripped a piece of cake from the golden roll, already mangled. He'd apparently partaken earlier. Green and purple and yellow granules of sugar skittered down into the box as he sunk his teeth in. Homey scents of butter, cinnamon, and vanilla melded with the coffee still in Binnie's hand.

The paper from the box explained that the cake was a King Cake and that inside the cake was a tiny plastic baby Jesus and that the tiny plastic baby Jesus was a choking hazard. Whoever found the tiny plastic baby Jesus in their slice of cake would have good luck for the day.

*Let them eat cake,* Binnie thought.

"Morning," she said.

"This cake is delicious and none of these clowns can have any of it," Baxter said. He devoured another buttery hunk, the crunch of decorative sugar faintly audible. Crumbs stuck to his lips.

A better person would say something, she thought, after a beat.

"Watch out for the baby Jesus," she said, finally, waving the greasy square of paper. "It's a choking hazard."

Baxter laughed but behind his eye twinkle she sensed a glimmer of misery, like he should be so lucky. He chomped again, swallowed, then coughed, as if the cake had gone down the wrong pipe. He turned away and coughed more, spittle and moist crumbs flying. Binnie thought that maybe some cake going down the wrong way would shake him out of himself. Like with Capra and his near-death experience changing his position on sick days. Baxter was nodding as if he was fine, despite the coughing. She'd thought *let them eat cake*, and now she thought, why not *let* him choke, he's miserable, he wants out—

Binnie whacked him hard on the back, because he was still coughing. *We're fucked anyway*, she thought, *all this waste for what, oil, baubles? Let them all eat cake, let them all choke on the plastic baby Jesus, all but the ladies on their sugar cleanse. Start afresh*—she shook her head and asked, as she whacked his back, her hand abuzz, "You okay?"

Baxter nodded but coughed harder, swayed forward. His face and ears were all red. He kept convulsing. He beat himself on the chest. Wheezed.

Index finger in the air, as if to excuse himself, he left the office. Where was he *going*?

"He all right?" asked Beatrice, poking up from her cubicle wall.

Binnie rushed after Baxter, slipping into the men's room before the door locked behind him. He hadn't made it to the toilet before he fell to his hands and knees, still purpling, rasping.

Stating the obvious, Binnie said, "Mr. Baxter, you're choking!" He would not lie down, so she straddled him piggyback and hugged him from behind and, remembering high school first-aid lessons, heaved both her fists into his diaphragm. Desperately, she squeezed, hoping to dislodge the baby Jesus. Shoving him all the way to the ground with no small measure of violence, she bore down again with her hands, with all of her weight, with gravity. Punched his gut with relish. Gritted her teeth in a contorted grin. His eyes widened.

In a gust of air deep from Baxter's lungs, the peach plastic Jesus flew out of his mouth and into a urinal with a dull, high-pitched *tink*. A caul of saliva made the doll slick. Baxter gasped, the color draining from his face. He touched his chest, rubbed his throat. He tried to stand, then thought better of it and sat.

"Are you all right?"

Still catching his breath, he made no answer, focusing his attention on the tile floor. Shook his head, ever so slightly. His face tinged verdigris. Something flashed across his face, as if he suddenly understood something completely and that understanding was utterly terrifying. He held out his hand, as if to keep Binnie at bay, as if to say, you've done enough, leave me to my humiliation. But the sickness didn't stop and Binnie didn't leave. His torso convulsed and torqued. He barfed into the urinal.

It was no small episode of vomit. Remnants of the previous night's dinner or perhaps midnight snack mixed with all that he'd consumed that morning sprayed against the porcelain. First the unnatural yellow, purple, and green of the King Cake. Then a tint of red, as if, in his stomach, something had torn: a bleeding ulcer. Binnie thought surely it would end here, surely that was all he had inside of his system.

But the last splatter. The last splatter glowed an unearthly hue. Turquoise, shimmering in the light, as if—as if—as if he'd stuffed his gullet with fistfuls of morpho butterflies.

An acrid odor of bile wafted past her nose.

By now, Beatrice was unlocking the men's room.

"Oh. My. God." She held the door open for Capra and Zaiman. Madeline peeped over their shoulders.

"Mr. Baxter, you're all green!"

Madeline stomped back to the office.

"Are you all right, Bob?" Capra edged closer to Baxter, who half-grunted. Sweat bubbled at his temples. Madeline rushed back with an ice pack wrapped in paper towels and applied it to his forehead.

"Let's get you out of here," said Zaiman, hitching him up. Baxter leaned on him, groaning.

Beatrice's brow crumpled at the unnatural mess in the urinal.

"We should call an ambulance," she said to Capra.

"Let me call my personal physician first. I don't trust emergency rooms."

Capra hustled back to the office. Beatrice surveyed Binnie, who averted her gaze toward the pool of blue flecked with the colors of Mardi Gras.

"I'll call for a janitor," Binnie volunteered. Beatrice nodded, stared at Binnie staring at the aftermath, and returned to the office, allowing Binnie to collect herself.

Alone in the men's room, with shaking torso and pincer-like fingers, she plucked out the baby Jesus and washed it.

*My pearl*, she thought. She cursed the lack of pockets on her dress, almost slipped it inside her mouth before finding a snug spot in the toe of her ballet flat.

❖ ❖ ❖

Baxter slumped in the vestibule. Madeline pressed the ice pack to his forehead. Zaiman paced the small area and Binnie zoomed by, trying not to limp with the stowaway Jesus in her shoe, pretending her task to call the janitor was as urgent as the emergency at hand. Capra hung up the phone, hollering at Beatrice as he hurried over.

"Call 911. My doctor says call 911."

Beatrice dialed.

Binnie snuck into the kitchen, found a Ziplock bag, and back at her desk transferred the doll inside of it. She hid the thing in a bottom drawer and beckoned a cleaning crew.

Task complete, she rested momentarily in a daze. Capra urged the curious to give Baxter space. The Zombie wandered back to his office, shaking his head. Zaiman paced in and out of the vestibule, dragging his hands down his face, exposing the red insides of his lower eyelids.

Rick stretched over the cubicle wall with a hint of excitement in his eyes. *Mirth?* In the Roman era, in the Colosseum, he'd be delighting in the Emperor's thumbs-down. *Finish him*, he'd holler before biting lustily into a hunk of bread. Binnie shot him down with a glare; his eyes slithered to his screen.

Binnie sat at her desk, listening to the bustle of the EMTs, their clipped orders, pronouncements of vitals.

"His vomit was blue," Beatrice told them.

"Could be food coloring," one said.

One of them assessed the mess in the bathroom.

"Whoa," came the sound of the cleaning crew with clanking slop buckets. The metallic whine of a gurney, the spastic sounds of walkie talkies, the slam of the door. Zaiman went with the ambulance; Capra called Baxter's wife, Kim. Binnie heard his report in snatches: allergic reaction, NYU Medical Center. He hung up and sighed. Capra padded to Beatrice. "If you're able to do so," he murmured, leaning on her cubicle wall, "please put together an accident report."

Grimly, Beatrice nodded.

Never in Binnie's life had she seen, in the context of the human body, that unearthly shade of blue. She trembled.

Let them eat cake.

Her mind had made itself known to her, and it was ugly.

❖ ❖ ❖

The office staff dispersed early that day. In the last rays of sunset, Binnie moped to Ess-A-Bagel for a cheap dinner. Inside, two Orthodox women, wigged and in pillbox hats, sat at a side table with a laptop and ledger. *A pound of walnut salad, a pound of tuna fish salad, twenty babkas,* one recited, while another checked off boxes. Binnie remembered the egg salad and black-and-white cookies Baxter had brought in the Saturday before trial, when he also gifted a silk scarf to Binnie and silk ties to Capra and Zaiman. His cheerfulness a thin mask over anxiety. Capra and Zaiman seemed vaguely disgusted with him, she couldn't quite understand why. A prickly response to his cloying plea for solidarity? Or something to do with their disapproval of his clients? Maybe it was simply an irritation with people who weaseled out of things, like paying what they owed.

She grabbed a cookie, sheathed in saran wrap. Over the cashier's head, a green-lettered box of napkins said Borax. A strange name for paper products, Binnie thought. *Two pounds white fish salad, two trays noodle kugel.* She chewed on the word Borax as she ate her bagel in the near-empty shop and pictured an assemblage—a barrel of shiny plastic fish next to a barrel of shiny shellacked egg noodles (why a barrel of noodles, what did that mean? it was eerie, but why?). The Borax logo behind them in the back of the box, giving everything a vaguely familiar quality. Was there a way of making it smell like childhood? What did childhood smell like? Ritz Crackers and the industrial-grade cleaning products of elementary schools. *Three pounds rugelach. No—four. Make it four.*

Industrial-grade cleaning products brought her back around to Baxter's vomit in the men's room. Her mind pivoted again. Borax was also roach poison, wasn't it? *Eight pounds Nova lox. Ten. Ten pounds Nova.*

The white bakery box had arrived Friday, the day of the exterminator's visit. *Did you forget the potato kugel?*

*Two trays.* She'd left the cake on Baxter's desk after he quit for the day. It marinated in insecticide fumes all weekend. *Two?* The women droned on. *Two. You got the Kosher beef salami?* And he'd eaten the cake. Had the exterminator warned about food? *Three two-pound logs.* Yes. He had. He'd asked if everything was well sealed.

She'd thought: let them eat cake. Even if she'd forgotten, maybe her subconscious had known exactly what was happening the whole time.

Binnie rose from her seat and dropped the half-eaten sandwich and cookie into her jacket pocket. *Wait,* said the women with the ledger. *We forgot the liverwurst.*

Binnie was out the door. In the excitement of the choking, no one had thought about the pesticide. Not even her. But she'd thought *let them eat cake,* and now the Borax logo at Ess-A-Bagel was a sign. Her breath grew ragged as she hurried home. Madeline had been out, and Binnie had put that cake in his office and left it there while the exterminator with his sweet smile sprayed the whole place. Monday morning, Baxter ate big hunks of King Cake, and she knew something was off but she said nothing; her mind had said, *Let them eat cake.* And now he was in the hospital spewing blue-green puke. Her hands shook as she turned the lock to her apartment.

Bent over her laptop, she googled "Borax" and "pesticide" and "consumption" and variations on those terms. Boric acid. That was it. "The main symptoms of boric acid poisoning," she read on Medline Plus, "are blue-green vomit, diarrhea, and a bright red rash on the skin." Bile rose in her throat and she swallowed it back down. She scrolled down a long list of other possible symptoms: blisters, collapse, coma...sloughing of skin. "Death from complications may occur as long as several months later. Holes (perforations) in the esophagus and stomach may result in serious infections in both the chest and abdominal cavities, which may result in death."

# Chapter Eleven

AT THE WINDOW of her studio, so sad and cramped yet so spare, a mottling of green, yellow, and sludge brown with specks of black haloed the edges of the glass. She knew she ought to tell Beatrice about the pesticide, but she was afraid. Was Baxter in for a slow, painful death? What constituted the "large amount" that Medline warned about? Children were most at risk, the page said, but the blue-green vomit was not promising. Not that a scientific description of amounts relative to body size would ease her horror. Her throat began to burn just thinking about the word *perforations*. Had she swallowed trace amounts? Had they *all*?

She called Gary. As the phone rang her mind spiraled back to the pause before the choking, the thought *let them eat cake*.

"Can you come over?" she asked, jettisoning greetings. "I'm too rattled to talk on the phone."

"Right now?"

"Right now, yes. Please, please?"

"You *do* sound rattled," he said. Something swished and zippered. His coat. "I can be there in an hour."

In fact, she worried about leaving records, divulging guilt. The cell phone company would surely have some kind of recording of their conversation in a vast archive somewhere. She wasn't so paranoid that she feared her apartment was bugged, nor did she see a need to line her walls with tin foil. But she did worry about phone calls. Oh, but that was crazy too! Maybe her fear of poisoning had begun before all this—maybe the years of glue and shellac in poorly ventilated spaces had damaged her mental faculties. Nervously, she paced, devouring stale saltines. The building's heat was still not working properly, so she kept her coat on. Across the hall, Carl blasted the evening news; the cadence of the reporting came through but no distinct words, no hints of a local man dying a horrible death by poisoned cake.

"What's wrong?" Gary asked when he arrived, frazzled, ears pink with cold. With her cheek to his cheek, eyes unfocused and directed towards the rough wood floor, Binnie told him about the cake, the pesticide, the vomiting, the turquoise hue. Gary pulled away, grasping her arms as if to steady her.

"The cake wasn't turquoise, was it?"

"No. Well. There were some green sprinkles, but not *blue*-green." She didn't yet mention that she'd googled the symptoms and they matched the effects of boric acid listed on Medline.

"No one thought of the pesticide? Binnie, you have to say something."

"Won't they see it in a blood test?"

"I don't know. You have to say something!" His grip on her arms tightened.

"I know. You're right." She wriggled away. A baby cockroach ran along the floorboards. She warmed her clammy hands by squeezing them under her arms. "What if I get fired?"

"What if he dies?"

"Okay. Okay. I have Beatrice's cell number in case of emergency. This is an emergency."

Gary's faced seemed to harden toward her. *Sensible shoes, maybe, but no sensible mind,* she thought, as the phone rang. *No sensible mind at all.* Beatrice picked up the phone, not pleased to hear from Binnie at 10:00 p.m. She sounded thoroughly drained, even more than when she'd started her punishing greens-and-lemon-juice cleanse-and-squats regimen. The modern version of the hair shirt. Binnie's whole body clenched. She tried to sound calm while still showing concern.

"How are you doing?" Binnie asked, hoping she wouldn't report any vomiting of her own.

"Me, I'm okay," said Beatrice. "Baxter, not so good."

"No?" Binnie's stomach lurched. She glanced at Gary, who knit his brows and nodded at Binnie as if to say, *do not chicken out.*

"He got to the ER, still vomiting, a high fever." She paused. "Don't share the details with anyone, please. His wife got there in time, but he—he didn't make it."

"*What?*"

Beatrice started sobbing. Binnie started shivering. She couldn't understand what Beatrice was saying. The receiver filled with wet mucus sounds. Binnie's throat constricted. The shivering grew violent and Gary stared at her, trying to understand what was happening. He twisted his face as if to say, *Aren't you going to say anything at all?* He could obviously hear Beatrice's sobbing through the telephone. It obviously sounded bad. His expres-sion slackened with the loss of hope. He held Binnie to quell the shaking and tilted his head toward her phone, trying to listen to Beatrice's side of the conversation. Binnie thought to ask whether the office would be closed in the morning but felt funny about it. Felt some relief at being able to realize that the question might be inappropriate.

Beatrice's voice quavered, rose in volume. "There's nothing we can do now."

"Jesus," said Binnie. There was a silence between them. "I'm speechless. I mean, Jesus."

"Yeah," Beatrice breathed. "We'll have to have some kind of announcement tomorrow morning. Capra will do it." Beatrice hung up.

"He's dead," Binnie said, disbelieving.

"Jesus," Gary said.

"That's what I said." Binnie lay down, coat and shoes still on, stared at the ceiling. Shuddered. Gary walked with purpose to her kitchenette, rummaging in the cabi-nets. He found Binnie's dusty bottle of Wild Turkey, which she'd bought as a college graduation present for herself. At the time she thought she'd finish it at crazy summer rooftop parties in Bushwick that she never ended up attending. He poured a finger into a glass, helped her sit up, and urged her to drink.

"One more should knock me out," she said, holding up the empty glass.

He rubbed her back while she finished the second drink. He pulled off her boots and coat and helped her into pajamas, thick socks, a hoodie which she drew tightly around her face, and a double blanket. *Let me hide forever in this cocoon,* she thought.

Gary stayed the night, holding Binnie. The shivers kept returning. He agreed, somewhat, that maybe at this point it didn't make sense for Binnie to say anything to anyone. Binnie lay in his arms as he drifted off and gently snored. The bourbon warmed her but didn't help her sleep. *Maybe he won't come back,* she'd thought, that Friday when he left early. Her gut had told her, on Monday, that something was wrong. *Let them eat cake. All but the ladies on their sugar cleanse.* She knew that cake was poisoned, and she let him eat it. She'd wanted all the lawyers dead!

She wriggled her face into the pillow. Was that it, then? Was she losing her mind at the tender age of 25? The thoughts kept coming back despite her attempts to push them away. *Maybe he won't come back. Let them eat cake.* She blinked up at the ceiling, adjusting to the dark, tracing the patterns of cracks in the plaster. The occasional streak of light zoomed by her window, throwing new shadows on the wall. Maybe he was out of his misery now. And now she didn't have to deal with him anymore.

*You are disgusting. Go find that cake in the trash and eat the rest yourself.* What of his wife, his daughter?

All night Binnie lay awake. She wasn't sure what time it was when a final question and answer drifted through her mind. *I killed Baxter?* I killed *Baxter.* I wanted him to die. *I fucking killed him. I'm a killer.*

❖ ❖ ❖

The next morning she held her breath in the elevator and tried to compose herself as she exhaled outside the unmarked door of the fund of funds. The door to CZB whined as she opened it. Madeline was at her desk, averting her gaze, and the Zombie was behind his door, coughing. At 10:15, Beatrice gathered Madeline, Rick, the Zombie, and Binnie into the conference room. She said the meeting would be brief, so there wasn't a need to sit down. They waited for the partners.

The sun shone in from Queens. Binnie squinted at the dust motes floating in the shaft of light that fell across the oak table. Her eyes felt sunken. She wanted to run out and get Beatrice a blood-dark beet juice to put roses in her wan cheeks. To help. To get away from what was about to be said.

Not long ago, in late August, just before the trial, everyone had convened here for cupcakes and plastic flutes of champagne on Baxter's birthday. It was a bigger crowd then, with Paul and Baxter's daughter doing her summer internship and, well, Baxter. Baxter asked Binnie to slice the enormous cupcakes in half so everyone could watch their girlish figures. The cupcakes, thickly frosted and goop-filled, disassembled under the plastic knife; Zaiman asked why she was butchering them; Capra said damn it, Mark, she's a paralegal, not a baker. Baxter laughed. She'd felt good hearing Capra call her a paralegal, even as she bristled against it. It meant she belonged. Was she going to say anything to anyone about the pesticide? She bit the inside of her cheek.

Capra trudged into the conference room, more sluggish than Binnie had ever seen him. Zaiman trailed behind him, eyes bloodshot, sallow skin a unique shade of chartreuse.

Capra cleared his throat and surveyed the room, as if he were searching for Baxter—Baxter's ghost. His face crumpled at the absence, and she could see in his eyes a flash of real, honest-to-goodness grief. He recomposed himself.

"We've lost a member of the Capra Zaiman family." He paused. "Last night, a little after nine, our Bob Baxter passed." Capra swallowed. "We're not certain of the cause of death. But his wife was able to be with him before he went." His head bowed slightly. "We're going to send out an announcement later today. Let's have a moment of silence for Bob." He bowed deeper.

Binnie's waxy pale hands folded in front of her. From the corner of her eye, she could see tears rolling down Madeline's cheeks. Sickly Beatrice remained stoic, already wrung out. Binnie avoided looking at Rick. She did not want to risk seeing glee. At the end of the silence, she looked at him anyway. His face was appropriately sober. Binnie exhaled through her nose.

"Are we gonna sue Verdier?" Rick asked Capra as they streamed out of the conference room. Capra cocked his head to the side and stared as if Rick had lost his mind.

"Not likely," he said, shaking his head and jangling his keys in his pocket, gazing down at 53rd Street.

❖ ❖ ❖

The atmosphere remained brittle. Capra and Zaiman met in the early afternoon. Not a decibel of raised voice slipped through the closed conference-room door. But after an hour, when Zaiman opened the door, he turned back to continue talking as he came out into the hall-way.

"What I don't get is the sudden—orthodoxy."

"All right. We're going in circles. Let's get back to work."

"Y'know, Bernie," he said, keeping his voice steady, "I really oughta just retire."

"Oh, c'mon, Mark," said Capra, deep voice breaking into an energetic shriek, then settling down again. "You say that every year."

"It's a little different now, isn't it?"

The lion's share of Baxter's work went to the Zombie. What kind of bonus would he get for *that*? Rick and Binnie and Madeline were to take turns going into Baxter's office and trying to make sense of the chaotic piles of paper, often covered in complex phone doodles. Nothing was to be thrown out. Beatrice filed the accident report and an outside accident investigator was set to come that day and ensure everything was on the up and up, that CZB wasn't some chronically unsafe workplace. Not that anyone worried Baxter's sweet wife would sue.

As Binnie puzzled through Baxter's piles, his heavy-handed zig-zag doodles and tiny, incomprehensible hand-written notes with the letters all shaky and clumped, the question of whether she'd been responsible collided with the vague notion that Baxter might have died somewhat intentionally. Was that possible? She'd felt that hitch, she'd had that thought as he was eating the cake: that he wanted it and *therefore* she should let him. Had he rushed to the bathroom to continue choking, gone off to die alone? Like an old dog? More important, wasn't it possible he knew about the pesticide? He had chosen the exterminator, after all. But if it had been a suicide, diligently planned, he might have chosen something more clean, more certain.

Perhaps he'd chosen the workplace to protect his family from witnessing his death or finding his corpse. An "accidental" poisoning would also leave the door open for a change of heart—you could ask for the stomach pump if you got cold feet. It would hide the fact of his suicide, keep his desire a secret. Did he feel stuck after the PanCorp loss? Did he sink his life savings and his kids' college funds into Madoff's scheme, lose them forever? Was he trapped in a job that he hated but had to go on with, because of a mortgage, wife, children...?

The vitamin supplements and pain relievers remained lined up at the back of his credenza. The potassium supplements were nearly gone.

What was it that he asked Beatrice to do—get an extra policy rider? On his life insurance.

What had Zaiman meant by "sudden orthodoxy"?

These questions did not relieve Binnie of the sense that she should have thrown out that cake, should have realized the possibility of danger as soon as he fell ill. Should have said something sooner. But, also, she wagered, if he'd planned to kill himself, he would've tried again with another method later.

Snooping was warranted. She had permission to be in his chair, rifling through his things. She opened Outlook, scrolling up and down for clues. Anything about the policy rider. Or Madoff.

There was an email from Capra's wife, Margaret, without a subject line. Emails without subject lines always seemed like red flags. *This message cannot be comfortably summarized*, they implied. She opened the thread. They'd made plans for coffee, but the details were vague. *I'll call you*, Baxter wrote. *thanks*, she replied. Neither bothered with punctuation, suggesting a certain level of intimacy. She searched for more. Of course Baxter wouldn't have emailed anyone about his plans or problems. Emails took him forever. He always preferred the phone. Less of a record.

Maybe it was nothing. Maybe Margaret was just planning a surprise party for Capra's birthday. She rummaged through the maelstrom of paper. There, beneath a response to the PanCorp appeal still awaiting judgment and an assortment of junk mail, was a copy of the policy rider. She skimmed it over and over, trying to make sense of it. It took some doing, getting her mind to glom onto the verbiage.

In the event of Baxter's accidental death, it said, Capra Zaiman Baxter LLP shall be an additional beneficiary. He'd signed it the day after Thanksgiving. Though that wasn't so long ago, the pages had been handled so often they were crinkled and worn. She left the document exactly as she'd found it, slightly askew at one corner of the desk.

So. Was CZB now in the money? She supposed it depended on the insurance company.

Under Baxter's desk, there was an open bag of pretzels. Binnie reached for a handful, almost began absently munching until she realized that these too might be tainted. She dropped the twists, retracted her hand from the bag. Rolled it up and took it out, pushed the pretzels deep into the kitchen trash, underneath old coffee grounds, empty bags of mixed greens, and thoroughly squeezed lemon halves.

After the violence of the choking and the Heimlich came the vomit. The vomit, too, came from the poison. She'd washed her hands with soap and scalding water until her skin pinked.

At some point, Baxter's wife would probably want to come in and bring home his personal effects—family photos he gazed at while lost mid-sentence in an email, the baseball bat he swung while deep in thought. Her voice on the phone had always been so calm and kind. The only thing she ever pushed on him, that Binnie could surmise, was that she wanted them to take a proper summer vacation. Not squeezed in at the last minute after agonizing over how to serve shady clients who did not pay their bills.

❖ ❖ ❖

The accident investigator interviewed each employee of CZB individually in the conference room, if only to briefly determine they'd not been in the office at the time of Baxter's demise. Binnie dreaded her interrogation. Should she come clean? Say she felt responsible? Would that mitigate any repercussions?

No. She had to believe that her fear was irrational. She had to assume it wasn't really her fault. She had to cover her ass.

"I won't take much of your time," the khaki-suited, tiny-chinned investigator said. Window washers dangled outside the window behind him, squeegeeing. Lines of water smoothed to nothing. Beyond the washers, the sky was impossibly blue.

"I came in yesterday morning," she told the investigator. "He'd apparently eaten one slice of cake already, maybe more. I don't know."

"He, meaning Mr. Baxter?"

"Yes. Then, on his next slice, Mr. Baxter—he started coughing, wheezing. I thought he was choking on the little plastic Jesus inside the cake."

"Wait, what?"

"There was a little doll. In the cake. It's a Mardi Gras thing."

The investigator carefully noted that.

"Do you have that doll? Is it around here somewhere?"

"No one else mentioned the doll?"

"I'm asking you."

"I'm not sure if it's still around. I think maybe the janitor mopped it up." She was saving it for a piece. The secret working title of the piece was "The Death of Baxter." She needed a different public title. The baby would be hidden, peek-a-boo style.

The investigator jotted that down and nodded, as if everything was starting to gel. "Continue, please."

"I tried to help, gave him the Heimlich. Then. This is so strange. He started vomiting. Maybe from the choking? That—that was the last time I saw him." Her eyes welled up. She wondered at their earnestness. Did she feel grief or was she performing? She had quite intentionally omitted mentioning the shimmering turquoise color he'd expelled.

The investigator softened, a perfunctory softening, she thought, and passed her a Kleenex. "I know this is difficult, but is there anything else you could share about what happened?"

This was her chance to confess, but she didn't bring up the extermination. The investigator had explicitly asked her about yesterday morning and she decided to keep her answer confined to yesterday morning. She paused, as if to reflect, then said no. The investigator thanked her for her time, said he might come back with follow-up questions, and left for the day. Free. For now.

❖ ❖ ❖

That night Binnie dined on beans straight from the can like a hobo. The slimy bottom greeted her spoon just as Gary called to see how she was doing.

"Bah," she said, lying down on the floor and setting the empty can of sludge by her head.

"Bah? Should I come over?"

"No," she said, elongating the "o" and turning her head the side, feeling her skull against the kitchen linoleum. The *nooooo* so childish. She picked up her head and thunked it on the floor. "I'm just laying here contemplating mortality." The plastic baby Jesus in the ziplock bag was now in her studio, inside her garbage bag of materials.

"I'm coming over right now," he said with a fatigued sigh. Perhaps he dreaded the commute and another encounter with all her hyperactive neuroses. But he knew it was best not to let her stew.

When he arrived an hour later, she was still on the floor. She heard her extra set of keys jingle outside and sat up, eager to burrow her head into the crook of his neck.

"You might feel better if you say something," he said, coaxing her onto the futon. "Get it off your chest." He stroked her back. She pictured the warmth of his hand penetrating her spine, seeping into her murderous heart.

"Get what off my chest? Do you think it was my fault?"

"No, but you're obviously miserable. I mean, if you brought up your concerns, wouldn't they appreciate your honesty?"

The room narrowed and darkened. She wasn't so sure. "I just have to get past this. I'll feel better with time."

Gary crinkled his brow. The sharp exasperation in his sigh surprised her. "You have to share things, Binnie. I don't necessarily mean now. But you have to share things of yourself to make people care. If you hold it all in, no one will ever know. And they'll stop asking, eventually— if they ever asked at all."

Binnie took a mental step backwards. What was he talking about? Not the law firm or Baxter. What was she keeping from him, what secrets did he sense? In their silence, she suddenly felt very *adult*. Was this what it meant to be an adult? Cautiously skirting implication in crimes?

Binnie reached for the bottle of Wild Turkey, now stored under the bed, and took a tiny baby swig of it.

They snoozed in their clothes for a few hours, then stripped at three in the morning and slept in a tangle. The morning proved difficult; they breakfasted wordlessly on peanut butter granola bars, crumbs scattering in the bedsheets. They moved robotically toward their jobs, as if on autopilot. She watched him descend into the subway beneath the Lipstick Building. Closed her eyes, queasy with the elevator's ascent.

❖ ❖ ❖

The raw atmosphere of the office seemed to have been cauterized overnight. The OilCo case jolted forward with the arrival of a box of discs containing hundreds of thousands of files. There was no mention of Baxter, yet he seemed to be at the back of everyone's throat. Once, in the vestibule, Madeline murmured to Beatrice, *I still can't believe it.*

Binnie wondered if Capra would have Beatrice send out an email about grief counseling. After 9/11, her college had offered everyone counseling. She'd gone to one session and all the therapist had said was, you seem to be doing okay, why don't you make a list of things you like about yourself.

There was no email about grief counseling. Instead, Capra asked Rick and Binnie to stay late. At least the extra work might distract her. Drown her mind in petrol.

She tagged "hot" documents in the discovery database. She spent more time with the Environmental Impact Statement than she was supposed to—it was irrelevant to the case, which was, like everything, squarely about money—hunting for ideas: flora and fauna. Sparrows and grouse skittering in Wyoming sagebrush.

Her mind drifted in and out of the database. Without Baxter, the OilCo case became Capra's entirely. Binnie wondered if that meant he got a larger share in the profits and whether there was any kind of secret guilty pleasure in that. Rick said Capra felt entitled to work in a relaxed manner because he'd worked ridiculously long hours in the first twenty years of his career—that he'd never learned to drive, bought a car, or had a real relationship until he made partner at a big-time firm at age forty. He met Margaret soon after that. Rick said that everyone at Capra Zaiman had it easy, that this was nothing like the sprawling white-shoe law firms downstairs where an eighty-hour week was the norm. *Implying we're wimps?* she wondered.

A deep smoker's cough rattled from the Zombie's windowless office. Every time he coughed, Rick sneered at Binnie, as if Dick's inability to work through the night over and over again and simultaneously be healthy was a major flaw in his being. As if Rick were the only one here who was truly fit to work, the only one worthy of survival. All he had to do was drink a cup of soup and gnaw on carrots while he worked and worked, giving CZB their full money's worth. She wondered if his sneers were an attempt at bonding with her through mutual hate. Or perhaps he was just desperate for the chance to sneer at someone, anyone. She kept her expression blank, which she knew irritated him to no end.

The day darkened quickly, but there was still plenty of work. Zaiman and Capra left at six, expecting Rick and Binnie to stay. Even the Zombie left before them. And it seemed like each of them wanted to be the last to leave. Did he want to be last to "win" at work or did he, like she, intend to meddle?

In the long hours steeped in the unpleasantness Rick exuded, she felt compelled to get on his good side, if only to make her life a tiny bit better, a tiny bit more livable. There had been moments when she'd thought they could form an alliance of sorts: that one time he offered her tea, for example. And every glancing invitation to schadenfreude, even though she dreaded those looks. His schadenfreude was much more malicious than Ellen's.

There seemed no better way to appease Rick than engaging in a little gossip. Gossip was the office's social mortar. Early in her time there, she'd invited him to lunch, hoping he'd be nicer afterward, but he'd shot her down, reminding her they couldn't both be out of the office at the same time. After that, she could never gear up to ask Rick if he wanted to grab an after-work drink. She did not want to open the possibility of his laughing in her face. But there was always gossip. And maybe he knew something more about Baxter.

The nauseating fluorescent lights were off; they worked under the warm yellow glow of their desk lamps. He'd stopped chomping on his infernal carrot sticks. Binnie sat taller in her seat. From behind their shared cubicle wall, as she lengthened her spine, Rick's red hair emerged, slightly sweaty against his pale forehead. Then his hazel eyes, the bridge of his nose.

"Did anyone say anything about Baxter's autopsy?" she asked.

Rick sat back, curious.

"Was there an autopsy?"

"Oh—I assumed there had been," Binnie said.

"I hadn't heard anything about that. Why would you assume that? I'd assumed it was some kind of freak allergic reaction."

"I guess I assumed autopsies were done as a matter of course," she said, trying to cover her tracks. "If no prior allergies were known." The words felt nonsensical and yet, upon reflection, retained logic. This scared her. She didn't consider herself the most logical person, and now reasonable explanations formed on her tongue a tad too easily.

The endless database stared back at her, long rows of coded documents sortable by date and whether something was "hot" or not. They were examining every email and every Board of Directors Meeting Minutes that contained the word "volume." Smug little missives about silica gel and cryo plant expansions and natural gas liquids and petroleum pipelines and "volumes" being excellent. Forceful flows of black oil rumbling beneath scrubby deserts. She suspected that every redacted sentence and phrase contained vital information. That everything they needed hid behind a solid black rectangle. The head honcho of the scheme had a face like a snapping turtle. She imagined a sprawling Texas ranch adorned with the pelts of polar bears and Siberian wolves, hunted from the perch of a helicopter with the ease of a sniping rifle.

"Did you have another theory?" Rick persisted.

*Don't do it, Binnie,* she thought. Be careful. Was it the guilt gnawing at her resolve? A spineless slug the size of her fist, slurping at her guts. She had the sense of losing control, veering off course. Just as she'd spewed logical ideas to cover her tracks, she would now spew self-incriminating words against her will.

She'd always thought Rick resembled a clean-shaven Raskolnikov, axe-wielding murderer of old ladies. But *she* was Raskolnikov in this situation, not him.

Sort of. That wasn't true, she reminded herself. She hadn't murdered anyone with an axe. Could she redact her thoughts, her memories, to stop this endless thought-sludge? Could she successfully redact these parts of her life?

"No. But, I mean, the office had been fumigated the previous Friday? We all had to clear out. And that cake that you think he was allergic to sat there all weekend. I mean, he ate two pieces of that cake and it had marinated in poison for two days. No one thought about that."

Almost imperceptibly, Rick grinned. "Did you tell the investigator?"

"Didn't even cross my mind until just now. I mean, you know how it is—things are quiet and then all of sudden a million things happen at once, and we're running around like headless chickens, and things fall through the cracks." Abruptly, she shut up. It was absurd. She felt better, having said it aloud, having heard herself say it. She felt better, for a moment.

Rick raised his eyebrows and smoothed his voice. "Yeah, okay. Too late, right? Spilled milk?"

Was he implying she didn't care? What was he implying? Oh god. She jumped out of her seat.

From the waist down, her body trembled—not a torso shudder like the night she'd called Beatrice. Her left leg and butt cheek twitched and she was sure that if it hadn't been for the cubicle wall, Rick would've noticed. Only once before had she shaken like this, the one time she had to speak before a crowd in college. She'd run out of the Rare Books reading room before she could barf on the display case inside of which sat a newly acquired illuminated manuscript, a jewel-toned chronicle of nobility. The *People* magazine of the medieval era.

Baxter's body had geysered hot iridescent butterfly vomit until he died. What the hell, Binnie.

She lowered herself back into her seat. Her pants felt damp. Was she sweating, or had she pissed herself? She didn't want to excuse herself, couldn't excuse herself now. She had to act cool, at least for a minute. She counted to sixty, staring at the marks on the screen, the barely comprehensible document numbers, scrolling up and down with no purpose. She knew she couldn't ask Rick not to tell anyone; that would only make things a hundred times worse. Maybe tomorrow she would call the investigator. Or tell Beatrice. Maybe tomorrow. Really, she should beat Rick to it.

In the ladies' room, Binnie splashed cold water on her face and neck, then rubbed her eyes and skin dry with a coarse paper towel. She filled her lungs as full as they would go, until it was painful, until she could feel the tips of them hitting the inside of her shoulders, and hissed out a slow exhale. When she returned to the office, Rick was gone, his desk lamp dark. Binnie's lamp was the lone light shining in the office. Goosebumps spread across her clammy body. Through the conference room windows, the yellow lights of Queens wavered and the red lights warning off airplanes en route to LaGuardia winked on, winked off.

# Chapter Twelve

A MACK TRUCK rumbled down First Avenue in the dark. Binnie wound herself tightly in her bed sheets. Lurid stories about Joseph Cornell came to mind, hints of criminality. A rumor she'd stumbled upon on the internet insinuated he'd been a pedophile, abusing the neighborhood children who wandered into his yard in search of toys. But that biography she'd been reading never said as much. In fact, it had been criticized for dancing around the subject, absolving him of this possible crime. In his fifties, Cornell began to hire college-age assistants, always female. One such assistant found copies of *Playboy* splayed open on his worktable. Shoe boxes filled with pink doll parts from Woolworth's sat on nearby shelves. A box for legs, a box for arms, a box for torsos. Naturally, this particular juxtaposition creeped her out—she'd quit that very day.

The gleam in Baxter's eye at the phrase *choking*

*hazard.* He'd known the exterminator had been scheduled—hadn't he? And if he'd known, he'd wanted it. And she let him. These ideas and images flickered through her mind in a blur, as if in a zoetrope. Why did she assign so much meaning to that gleam?

The alarm blared at seven. Binnie smacked it off and slept until almost ten. A cold shower will shock me awake, she thought. In the tiny stall, she dropped the economy-sized shampoo bottle on her foot, sliced her leg open with the razor, and bumped her elbow into the wall.

"Oh, Binnie!" her landlady said as she rushed down the stairs. "I'm glad I caught you. You forgot to the pay the rent this month."

"Yes," she said. "Yes, I'm late for work, but thank you very much for the reminder." Binnie edged past her on the narrow stairs. She would have to continue forgetting until pay day. The hair on her landlady's chin, long and wiry, glinted in the hall light. She thought of Raskolnikov murdering an old lady, just to see if he could.

"You still have soap in your hair. Are you going out like that?"

"What are you, my mother?" Binnie stomped back up the stairs and shoved her head under the kitchen sink, finger pads kneading her scalp. Sped to the Lipstick Building with wet but soap-free hair.

"Sorry," she said to Madeline and Beatrice, dumping her bag under her desk and wrenching off her coat.

She woke up the computer and poured herself black coffee, spilling some on the counter. Baxter's name on the mug taunted her; she wondered if the partners would leave it there to honor his memory or if one day in the future, Beatrice would smash these mugs for her garden too, just as she'd done with the old mugs, when there'd been a fourth named partner who'd left. The new mugs would instead say Capra Zaiman. It reminded her of the Pharaohs who'd demolished the likenesses of their vanquished rivals. No, that wasn't an apt metaphor. But the erasure seemed significant. She dumped her coffee in the sink, as if the name on the mug had tainted it, and poured more into a paper cup that came from a sealed plastic sleeve, and wiped down the mess she'd made on the counter.

After the chaotic morning, she tried to approach Madeline quietly. "Is it my day again for cleaning Baxter's office?"

Madeline jumped in her seat. "Binnie. I didn't hear you there."

"Sorry." Binnie's hand shook as she drank her coffee. "I was just offering to do Baxter's office if you didn't feel like it today."

"Thanks. I—"

Capra's keys jangled in their direction. "Binnie. Glad you decided to join us today."

"So sorry. Just overslept a smidge." She giggled nervously and backed away from the tight quarters of the reception area, feeling an awkward heat between Capra and Madeline. The odd expression on his face was not comforting. She patted her head. *Damp hair is a sign of unprofessionalism*, a garbage article on LinkedIn had once declared. Maybe he was just looking at her weirdly because she looked like a drowned rat.

She gravitated toward Baxter's office, which appeared neater today. All the files that had been on his desk, including the policy rider, were gone. The files that had been on top of the credenza were gone. The pain relievers and vitamin supplements were gone. She checked the wastebaskets: empty. His personal effects, too, were gone: the family photos, the baseball bat. Gone, gone.

She constructed a banker's box and pulled out a file drawer, rolling up her sleeves. Rick walked by the open door and when their eyes met she could not help but read this sentence in his glare: *You'll be gone too, soon enough.*

The objects in her mind formed a gaudy, sinister assemblage: sparkling King Cake, a skull-and-crossbones representing roach poison, a shimmering turquoise puddle, a bony-hipped pinup girl. Without Baxter's wholesome family staring at her from framed photographs, she felt emboldened to meddle further.

His personal banking statements. Investments.

He *had* invested in Madoff. Becca must have been skiing in the Swiss Alps when he found out, she imagined. *It's all downhill from here!* Was he paying for Tufts out of pocket or had they taken out loans? What about the Escalade he'd gifted her when she graduated from high school? And what could Binnie do with any of this information? Was there anything *to* do?

❖ ❖ ❖

As soon as she returned to her desk, Madeline popped up, pulling on her coat.

"I'm outta here," she said. "See you tomorrow."

"You're not coming back?"

Madeline shook her head and waved, the big cuff of her coat drooping down to reveal a solid black eight-pointed star on the inside of her wrist. This made Binnie catch her breath. Was the universe providing a clue? To what? The solid blackness like a redaction, the star's eight directions too many ominous possibilities.

"Is that a new tattoo?"

Madeline admired her wrist, smiled, and nodded, slipping on an enormous pair of sunglasses. Like an incognito movie star.

Beatrice asked Binnie, "Where've *you* been?" The door slammed behind Madeline, and the phone rang. Beatrice sucked her tongue, left Binnie to her duty. Binnie lingered over Madeline's desk as she answered the phone. On her computer screen: 50 Astonishing Photos of the Milky Way. Photo 50 of 50: a thick, luminous swirl, ejaculate of the cosmos.

Capra and Zaiman both left early. Binnie ducked into Capra's office. Maybe she'd find the original pinups. Maybe she'd find a clue. *As a small treat*, she joked with herself, *you can steal one*.

Her eyes darted over each tower of files on the credenza, on the floor, on the chair facing his desk. She shook the mouse; if someone inquired, her story would be simple. Capra had asked her to pull up an email—he'd done that before, even though he owned a Blackberry. In fact, she'd get that same email if need be. Something about a State Insurance Commissioner. But now she searched for HoneyBear6969@gmail.com. Nothing. Should she figure out how to clear the search history? Or would that be even stranger, more suspicious? She should have just typed the letter H to see what would pop up. Stupid. Her eyes darted again around the room.

In the bookcase across the office, wedged between two red leather tomes, an outcropping of paper. Like a finger in the crack of doorway, beckoning: *come hither.* Binnie x-ed out the search box, went to the shelf, and tugged out glossy photos. Colorful 8x10s: Georgina. Anyone could have come in here, scanned these photos, and returned them with Capra having no idea.

How was she going to prove it was Rick? If she confronted Capra, he'd have to ask Rick, and Rick would never come clean. Should she save the photos as leverage in case Rick said something about her and the roach poison? The firm should not allow such images in the office, not stuck on a shelf more or less in plain sight. To leave copies on an employee's computer? That was harassment.

Impulsively, she picked up a file folder and slipped one photo inside, without looking to see which one it was. She settled back in at her desk, snuck the file in her shoulder bag, acted busy. Something pounded in her ears. The refrigerator, the Xerox machine, the computers hummed.

❖ ❖ ❖

Outlook notified Binnie of a new email. That blue rectangle—she'd never considered it ghostly until now. The message was from Honey Bear. "I know what you did," it said. That was it. No subject line. No salutation. No signature. No allusion to Baxter. Or roach poison. Or murder. No allusion, even, to the pinups that had been sent from her work email to Honey Bear. Just that one cheesy slasher-flick sentence. *I know what you did.*

She created a separate folder, "H. Bear," and stored the message there, within the nest of another folder, "Misc." Should she respond? Imprudent. She should rummage around on Rick's computer to see if he'd used that Gmail account. All she'd have to do is open Gmail and type "h" in the login to see if Honey Bear came up. How much snooping can you do without getting caught?

Her gut rejected spying on Rick's computer. Capra was one thing—he got so many emails each day there was little chance of his noticing something amiss. Rick, on the other hand. Rick was organized, shrewd. And ready to skewer her. Of that she now felt confident. The imminent skewering was palpable.

More and more she gravitated toward a plan that would either succeed or fail spectacularly. Bring the pinups to Capra's attention. Complain of a hostile workplace. Maybe, even—*maybe*—get rich through a settlement. Because it *was* a hostile workplace, with these uncomfortable, inappropriate photos just sitting around, intruding on her psyche. And if that worked, then maybe she could live the artist's life she'd always wanted.

And, this was not a small thing: if she tried to stay objective and rational, she knew she had nothing to do with Baxter's death. She had to keep exonerating herself on that front. It was sickening to keep thinking she'd put him out of his misery, over and over again till the thought wore a rut in her brain.

She half-expected Honey Bear to read her mind and email a goading message. *Go on and try that. See how far it gets you.* She had to beat Honey Bear. Beat that nasty pipsqueak to a pulp. Metaphorically, that is.

❖ ❖ ❖

At home that night she celebrated her plan with a glass of her new best friend, Wild Turkey. She finished a finger of it before shakily pulling out the folder with the glossy photo of Georgina. It was the one with "I love you, Bernie" written in blue gel on her belly. It had weird repercussions now, what with Madoff. But also: if this was a true declaration of love, was this the worst theft possible? Would Capra miss this photo especially? Would he care? Georgina would. Margaret. Margaret would care in an altogether different way.

She loomed over her work table, cleared except for Aunt Ruby's perfume bottle and the installation sketches. If she was to survive this life drama, the possibility of maybe actually one day succeeding as an artist was a lifeline. Even if she had to serve prison time for manslaughter—was that actually possible???—no, banish the idea—she would have something to look forward to. The plastic baby Jesus was the perfect little bauble to build a diorama around, the perfect complement to the little boy with the ice cream smile. Maybe she should develop a triptych of sorts. Birth—the baby; Sex—the pinup, altered somehow, perhaps with a Mardi Gras mask over Georgina's face; Death—"Infection."

Gary texted. When she didn't respond, he called.

"I don't know, Gary." Binnie swirled the amber liquid in her glass, ice cubes clinking. "I think I need to be alone tonight."

She didn't want to tell him about the photos.

She didn't want him to dissuade her.

"Okay," he said, voice sagging.

She turned away from the table. For a second, she considered consulting Ellen. Those late-night chats in college. She was the keeper of secrets. She might have ideas.

"Tomorrow? I'll be in a better place tomorrow."

"Sure," he said. "Tomorrow. Love you."

"Love you too."

She set the phone face down on the table, caught her reflection in the dark window.

Her face crumpled.

"Damn it."

❖ ❖ ❖

She ascended the cabbage-scented stairway, lips trembling. Arlene, in an ankle-length flannel nightgown, opened the door, eyes widening. She pulled Binnie inside, where the heat immediately overwhelmed.

"Mom."

"What? What happened? Did you get fired?"

"No—"

"Oh, thank god. Take off your coat. What's wrong?"

They sat on the sofa in the living room. Binnie wiped her nose with the back of her hand. Down the hall, her father snored.

"I don't know where to start."

A gap-toothed portrait of a six-year-old Binnie hung on the wall, her wild, wispy curls shorn into a pixie cut. Fallout from a safety-scissors self-styling experiment.

Arlene patted her hand.

She mentioned Baxter's death.

"Oh no!"

And the pattern of fired people. The pattern of Rick picking them off.

"Oh my."

And the pinups.

"How odd." Arlene clucked her tongue. "Honey, honey. If this guy is trying to get you fired, why would he give you this gift of the pinups?"

"Huh?"

"Why would he sabotage himself like that?"

"I don't know. Because he doesn't think I'd do anything? Because he thinks I'm scared and he wants to torment me?"

"It's gotta be this guy Capra's wife. Or another girlfriend."

"Wait, but why?"

"You're a young lady. You know how things go. I bet it's a veritable harem over there."

"Ew, Mom. You read too many romance novels."

"If this were a romance, you'd be married already."

Binnie picked at lint on her sleeve. "I hate to say it, but maybe you're right. About the ick factor, not the married part."

"Of course I'm right. You say something to those lawyers. They'll crap their pants. You'll be fine."

"But what about my job?"

"Well, find a new one."

"In the meantime?"

"In the meantime suck it up. You can't afford otherwise."

Binnie bit her lip. "But it's terrible! What about me? What about my art?" Binnie knew these questions would not persuade her mother to offer better advice.

Arlene shook her head. "Oh, honey. You always wanted to do something different. Remember your fourth grade Purim party?"

Binnie grunted and rubbed her eyes with the heels of her hands, generating white-blue splotches beneath her eyelids. Arlene liked to bring up this Purim party in Binnie's moments of distress.

"Remember? You said, 'Everyone wants to be Esther. Esther, Esther, Esther. That's boring! I'm gonna be Vashti.'"

"Uh huh."

"Vashti the rebel. Vashti who refuses to dance for the king. But Vashti gets killed! Esther knows better. She games the system. She saves the day."

"Yeah."

"Remember how disappointed you were, when the girls didn't get your Vashti idea?"

"This isn't making me feel any better, Mom."

Arlene stroked Binnie's head. "What I'm saying is, one of these days, you'll learn how to game the system." She shrugged. "Or you won't. That's life."

Binnie stuck her head under the comforter and screamed into the pillow, which tasted faintly of prune jam.

# Chapter Thirteen

MAYBE QUITTING COFFEE would help quash the waves of panic, Binnie thought the next morning. She bought plain green tea from a cart, but by the time she took a sip, it tasted like metal and fish. On her desktop, a new PDF taunted her. Madeline, Beatrice, and the Zombie murmured in the vestibule. Capra and Zaiman toiled in their separate quarters. Suddenly, Zaiman shot out of his chair and closed his office door; a faint noise came through, like a strangled sob. Binnie's hand flew to her neck in sympathy. Despite all his hectoring of Baxter, or maybe because of it, the two men had often remarked they were like brothers. Capra jerked up his head, dialed into Zaiman's office.

"Are you okay?" She could hear his voice both down the hall and on Zaiman's speaker phone. She couldn't hear Zaiman's reply. Capra hung up, shuffled down the hall, slipped into Zaiman's office.

Rick's pale forehead, framed with faintly damp red locks, was visible over the cubicle wall; on his side, a tinny broadcaster muttered about the NASDAQ. They peered over the wall at each other but said nothing of Zaiman's apparent sob.

Secure in the location of her nemesis, Binnie exhaled. Double-clicked on the new PDF.

There was Georgina again, this time in a Polaroid. Topless, g-stringed, sporting thigh-high black leather boots and a glittering 8-inch strap-on. Twisting at the waist to face the camera, she perched one small, stiletto-heeled foot on the peach buttocks of a man—his head was not in the frame. She held up a riding crop with palpable relish. So very different from the woman with the tremulous voice that Binnie had encountered in November!

Binnie coughed to hide her involuntary gasp, moving that photo to the nest in the Paralegal folder. Despite the heart palpitations it induced, she had to hand it to Georgina: this last photo suited her best. On the other side of the cubicle wall, Rick typed feverishly. And now, again, the hated blue rectangle of Outlook. Honey Bear. *I know what you did.* Delete delete delete. Abort. Delete.

Binnie jumped up and rounded the corner toward the file room in an attempt to see, from afar, if Rick was, in fact, Honey Bear. If he was, though, he'd already clicked out of Gmail and back to the OilCo database. She circled around the cabinets in the center of the room and grabbed an expandable file at random. She passed Madeline on the way back to her desk, but Madeline avoided her eyes. Capra returned to his office. Zaiman kept his door shut. The Zombie plopped a file on Binnie's desk. As she headed for the copy room, she heard Rick say, "Mr. Capra, can we meet in your office?"

A door closed gently. Beatrice inhaled audibly.

"If you really want to murder someone," the Life Science teacher had said, "give them an extremely high dose of potassium. Potassium naturally increases in the body upon death, so it's a lethal agent impossible to detect." Death by super-banana. What the hell was Baxter doing with potassium supplements? She dared not google it.

The air seemed to crystallize; in the conference room, dust motes floated. Sparkling. Faintly squeaking. She slipped a stack of papers into the velobinder to be punched, then threaded plastic teeth into the punched holes and sealed the binding. Chemical stink and melting warmth rose as the machine buzzed.

❖ ❖ ❖

Her phone rang that afternoon. The red light flickered a moment, the ringer insistent despite its low volume. Not the shrill of an outside call but a discreet beckon from inside the office. Would it be Honey Bear, calling from the file room? *A sotto voce accusation: I know what you did.*

"Can you see me, please?"

Capra was on the line, unusually subdued, so that she could not hear any echo of his voice coming from the direction of his office. She wanted to ask why. Instead she said okay.

That question, *can you see me, please*, always made her apprehensive. But if he was really mad he'd storm over to her desk, indignant, and ask, with a voice like a hatchet, "Whatever happened to...?" and she would have to calmly explain what had happened. Once she'd thrown Madeline under the bus, said Madeline had sent a document to the wrong recipient; Madeline told Capra she must've gotten confused. This was well before the chaos of the morning Baxter died. It seemed insignificant in light of the tragedy.

But that subdued voice. *Can you see me please.* What about the strange tone he'd taken with Madeline before the holidays, about enjoying her bonus? Was this some-how the same? Was it him sending the photos all along? Like when Cornell left *Playboy* out for his assistant to see? Capra was smarter than that, she kept telling herself. It didn't seem possible. But lately the realm of possibility had grown exponentially. It gaped, an abyss. An eight-pointed star. Being smart might be beside the point. Being power-ful might be the point. She licked a finger and turned her notepad to a fresh page, picked up her favorite pen. You'll be fine, she told herself. With deliberate steps she walked to Capra's office, but the steps, she hoped, were not so deliberate as to give pause to anyone watching. She channeled an image of poise.

"Close the door and have a seat," said Capra. Uh oh. Well. That was a first. She closed the door carefully, as if the gentleness would help her somehow.

A green-tinted goat flew across a Chagall print on the wall, tiny crescent-shaped whites in its eyes. It wasn't a whimsical goat. It was white-eyed with goat fear. Dizziness wavered through Binnie's head as she sank into a chair. She wanted to plunge her face, ostrich-like, into a pit of Jujyfruits.

Capra rummaged for the right words. It occurred to Binnie only now that this man named Capra had a painting of a goat on his wall. At another time, this would have made her giggle. She widened her eyes and stared at the floor, to prevent, even now, giggling. Lunatic.

"I'll just get to it," he said finally, gaze steady. "There's some serious charges against you in this office." Heat streaked through the core of her body. Slicks of sweat formed on her forehead, the front of her neck, armpits, backside, crack. The spaces between her toes. She said nothing. Swallowed. "I wanted to talk to you alone and give you a chance to tell your side of the story."

*My side. Okay, my side. What's my side?* "What do you mean, charges?" She softened her voice so as not to sound defensive. Simply...inquiring, concerned.

"I won't go in to who said what. But, the...suggestion... is that you've grown careless in your work. That you have not been as *reliable* as we've come to think, as you've appeared, that you've become very—distracted."

"*What?*" She leaned forward, pulled back. She urged herself not to be rash. "Did Rick say that?"

Capra paused. She took his silence for a yes.

"It was an *accident*, Mr. Capra. If I had known and if I had been able to, I would've pumped his stomach myself.

Jesus." She snapped her palm tight against her mouth, elbow rammed into her knee. In a picture that came to eye level, Capra and his wife grinned at Machu Picchu.

When she looked back at Capra, he appeared alarmed. "What? What are you talking about?"

"Mr. Baxter. The cake. The exterminator."

Margaret Capra. Margaret had emailed Baxter. Did Baxter tell her about Georgina? Did she then exact atonement for what he knew?

Wait—if Honey Bear was Margaret—did she think Binnie was *Georgina* and send the photos as evidence of her transgression? Or did she think Binnie herself was with Capra—another liaison? Margaret never came to the office, so maybe she didn't know. Maybe she envisioned the same harem Arlene envisioned. Disorientation sprouted in Binnie's mind, a gangly web of mold-green muck.

To Binnie's casting about, Capra said, "Please try and stay calm. Let's backtrack. Why don't you tell me what happened, from your point of view?"

Binnie swallowed. Mentioning the pinups now would just confuse him. He spoke and listened in a linear, methodical way. Deviations from the linear always incited his ire. Begin at the beginning. Capra picked up his fountain pen, ready to jot notes.

"Okay. Verdier's cake arrived Friday, around ten. Mr. Baxter asked me to put it on his credenza, then left early. Toward the end of the day, we're scrambling, busy with a heap of last-minute projects. You know we had those twelve briefs to send out. The cake is the last thing on my mind. At five, the exterminator comes in, tells us to clear out, and we do. He sprayed pesticide all over the place. Monday, well, you know what happened Monday. Mr. Baxter ate a slice of cake, choked on the baby Jesus, and got sick. I gave him the Heimlich. I saved him. Nearly."

Capra noted everything, pen gliding across his legal pad. How he enjoyed the fluidity of that pen.

"Yes," he said, gravely. "In the moment of the emergency I didn't think of it, but I wanted to commend you on that. On the Heimlich."

Binnie exhaled. Did that absolve her of anything? It occurred to her now that "I forgot" about the pesticide might not be a suitable defense when a matter involved death. Fuck. But—she had no experience with criminal law, and, anyway, what about everybody else who "forgot"?

"Mr. Capra—can I ask? Was there an autopsy?"

"Kim refused one, on religious grounds."

"I thought Mr. Baxter wasn't so religious." *I don't get the sudden orthodoxy,* Zaiman had said. Kim was Catholic, she'd understood. Did they object to autopsies too?

Capra pressed his lips together. "It's what Bob would have wanted, Kim said."

Would now be the time to mention the photos? *Speak now or forever—*She could at least insinuate something about Rick's pattern of having people fired. He had been at CZB for nearly five years. No junior paralegal had stayed with CZB longer than a year or two during Rick's tenure; the many additions to the red Paralegal binder, each with their dated Departure Memo and instructions and advice for their successors, showed that. Binnie had been at the firm about nine months. Her time could be nearly up. Capra would take Rick's word over Binnie's. Had he gotten each of her predecessors fired? Or coerced them, somehow, into quitting?

There was the part-time contract attorney. Paul. Rick had said he wasn't pulling his weight. And before her time there was that paralegal he'd caught snorting coke in the bathroom. *Oh, I got him good*, Rick had said.

Maybe, for Rick, it was win-win-win. Baxter dies in extravagant fashion; Binnie quits or gets fired; Capra implodes. Maybe for him, it was like a video game.

"The point is, I wasn't negligent," Binnie said. "I think..." A drop of sweat fell from her neck to the brown wool of her lap. "I think someone in the office is trying to set me up." She pulled a loose curl behind her ear.

Capra set his pen down. He did not seem to think this madness was worth recording. Binnie grew light-headed.

Was Rick banking on her being too timid to mention the photos? Maybe he underestimated her. *Maybe he expected her to be too afraid to say anything.* And indeed, if Honey Bear were not Rick but Margaret, the intimidation factor remained valuable. Who was Margaret to blame Binnie for Capra's lechery?

*Beat Honey Bear.* Out with it.

"Listen," she said. "I'm not sure what anyone's told you, but there's something going on. Something strange has been happening."

Capra picked up his pen. "Yes?"

"There were—strange files on my desktop. Maybe as a prank? They made me very, very uncomfortable. Unsafe, even. I don't know who did it, but someone scanned— inappropriate pictures."

"Inappropriate."

"Yes. Of—Georgina. Boudoir photos."

Capra's skin tomatoed. He glanced over Binnie's head, through the window into the rest of the office. His eyes flitted upward at the blinds, as if he wished to draw them down, but of course he couldn't. He regarded Binnie. Her legs trembled.

"What do you mean?" The blood drained from his face. "Are you trying to change the subject?"

"No—"

"Don't change the subject."

"I, uh." Binnie's head buzzed. Her face felt cold and hot at once. She glanced toward the bookshelf where the photos had been stuffed. They were gone. "Whether it was intentional or careless, I am—extremely—uncomfortable."

Capra pressed his lips together, tapped his pen on his legal pad, and exhaled through his nose.

Binnie stared at his notepad. Was he going to write any of this part of the story down? He seemed to notice her questioning this. Then, he did it. He wrote something down. This encouraged her. "Rick is up to something," she spat.

"What makes you say that?"

"Well, for one, he's always bragging about paralegals he's gotten axed." A faint, bitter chuckle slipped from Capra's mouth. The bitterness suggested defeat, like Rick knew too much about Capra and was already lording something over him. "You say I've been careless, but how can I work with, with pornographic material shoved in my face?"

"Is this about the Chapter 7 case?"

"It's about there were pictures of your *girlfriend* on *my* computer."

The clarity of the statement shocked her. Capra sat silently, taking it in. The phone rang and momentarily he looked unsure, but he picked up on the third ring, because he could not resist. He never could let a phone ring. Still, he indicated Binnie should stay. So she did.

After a minute, the mold-green muck of her mind began stirring. Capra hung up, and she asked, "So what's happening? Am I getting fired?"

"Not—necessarily."

"Not necessarily? So I might get fired?"

Capra relaxed. His voice, grown brittle, regained energy. As if the mention of firing brought back the issue of carelessness for him, which brought back the issue of Baxter for her, which made the mention of the photos disappear. As if he could steamroll over them.

"It's serious, Binnie. The carelessness. The unreliability. And now we have to take into account...your computer. Do an internal investigation. Comb the files. This is a serious accusation you've made. So in the interim, I think you're going to have to take some time off. I believe that's what's best. Paid leave."

"Huh." The moisture on her neck and back grew clammy. She'd fucked up. Paid leave? Plenty of time to scrub her computer clean. She lowered her eyes. There was the photo Binnie had taken home. But admitting to theft was problematic. And despite everything that was happening, she thrilled at *using* it in a piece to show Alexis. What would he have said if she'd never brought up the pinups? Or Baxter?

"I never expected anything like this to ever happen." Her voice fried; she tried not to cry in front of Capra. Crying could render her sympathetic—or just pathetic.

Capra handed her a tissue. "Take the rest of the day off. Let me walk you out. Beatrice will give you a call later."

As they passed the Chagall print, the sheen in the eyes of the green flying goat hinted now at a fear of destruction. An investigation? She was ruined. Capra hovered beside her cubicle to supervise her gathering her purse and coat. She didn't want to look at any of the others, their dead-eyed stares. She was just fodder for future office lore. Despite herself, she looked. Zaiman's gaze was pained, askance. Rick's malicious. Dick, trudging toward the coffee machine in the kitchen, jaw working on a ball of gum, seemed indifferent. A roach scuttled past his shiny black shoes; he stepped around it.

Wait, but had Capra said investigation? Or criminal investigation? No, he'd said *internal* investigation. Right? It was too late to ask. Beatrice appeared and put a hand lightly on Binnie's shoulder, and the two women rode the elevator down to the lobby together.

"Beatrice, are you going to help me out on this?" Her throat constricted.

Beatrice's expression betrayed nothing. "I'm sorry this is happening. Take care of yourself."

At the security gate, Beatrice asked for Binnie's ID. Binnie wanted to ask why Rick was ruining her life. She handed over the ID and tried to act calm and sane, and at the same time indignant, but not so enraged as to be considered a danger.

"Thanks. We'll call you, okay? Be available by phone."

Outside, the air was brisk. A hint of spring wafted up from the south, plunging Binnie into a deep melancholy. "Moored on Third Avenue." She imagined a doll version of herself dressed in a little brown wool suit, slumped on the edge of a planter empty of flowers, just a little pile of dirty snow to keep her company. The rush hour crowd thickened. What if mentioning the pinups had made everything worse? What if Arlene was dead wrong? Binnie's mom trusted a system that was falling apart—had expectations of financial security in old age—expectations that somehow things would work out, that Binnie's "leverage" would mean she'd be taken care of.

No one would be taken care of.

She flipped open her phone.

*Srsly need a drink*, she typed to Gary.

He wrote back immediately: *Margaritas in 45.*

She took the F train to Brooklyn. F for Felon. F for Fuck-up. F for Failure.

At least it was Friday; she had forty-eight hours to regain her wits. Or forty-eight hours to plunge deeper into uncertainty. She bawled all the way to the restaurant; most people scooted away from her, but one brave lady handed her a packet of tissues before debarking. She clutched the packet gratefully, a morsel of sympathy onto which she could cling.

❖ ❖ ❖

The cavernous dark of the Mexican joint on Fifth was a balm. She flopped onto the vinyl seat, drained.

"Can we do a pitcher of sangria instead?"

Sangria felt more appropriate than margaritas. Maybe it was the reference to blood. The salt in a margarita reminded her of mummies. Blood equals life; salt equals a corpse.

"Of course, whatever you like."

Sullenly, they devoured a basket of warm tortilla chips.

"Are you going to tell me what's wrong?"

"I don't know that I can. I mean, I guess I can. I think. But I don't think you can tell anyone." She drank. An apple chunk bobbled against her lip. "Remember when you came over the other night, the emergency with Baxter?" Gary nodded gently, brow crinkled. "Well, I seem to be getting in trouble for it. Maybe."

Gary's eyebrows slowly uncrinkled. "Really?"

"Uh, I was escorted out of the office today."

"Like, forcefully?"

"No, not like that. Though Beatrice did put her hand on my shoulder. Anyway. I had to hand over my ID card. I have to take time off. They're—investigating."

Gary's head threatened to pop off his neck. "Should you...get a lawyer?"

Binnie wiped her sangria mustache. "Ugh. Maybe. I don't know how I'm supposed to afford that."

"Wait, are you getting sued? Or arrested? What exactly happened over there?"

"I don't know!" She plunked her head on the table. It smelled like stale beer. "I might get fired, at least. They said something about carelessness, about me being unreliable. " She thought about Ruby's apartment. Idiot, idiot, idiot.

Gary hedged. "You're very upset."

Ah, therapist mode. "I appreciate the empathy, Gary, I do." She grabbed his hand; he put his other one on top. She rested her forehead on the warm pile of hands. "What I need is problem-solving."

"Okay. Maybe Gerta would take you back?"

Binnie lifted her head up just enough to scowl. "I kind of screwed her over, didn't I, leaving at the last minute?" Her head shot up, a surge of anxiety propelling her. "Seriously, what if I do go to jail?"

"That's ridiculous. I'm sure you're not going to jail."

"Gary! I'm serious. I visited Riker's Island on a high school field trip. They didn't take us to the women's unit because it was too dangerous. I'm gonna get shanked in the kidney." Ice picks, nail files, dull knives. The Corrections Officer conducting the tour showed an elaborate collection of homemade, clandestine weapons. The young men in holding cells had hooted at her criminal psych class, thinking they were in a Scared Straight program. The older inmates who'd been inside for much longer were more subdued. Resigned.

"Breathe," Gary said, pouring each of them more sangria. "You might be tormenting yourself for nothing. We should order dinner. Let's take it to go, and you can tell me exactly what happened."

Binnie nodded, chewing on wine-flavored ice.

❖ ❖ ❖

Gary checked to make sure his apartment was empty.

"No one's here. Let's eat at the table." The few times they'd dined at his place before, it was on the relative island of solitude and cleanliness that was his bed, the one clear spot in his room apart from a sort of triangular path between the bed, the door, and the dresser. "You can go over what happened. Maybe start back from when Baxter got sick. Or whenever. Whenever's the beginning."

The scent of melted cheese from the enchiladas sickened Binnie. She couldn't talk about it and eat. She pushed the container away.

"So. Here's what I think happened." Her words slurred, the half pitcher of sangria tugging them down. Her cried-out eyes felt sunken. "Friday at ten or so, Baxter gets a package from a client. This big white bakery box. I leave it on his credenza and he leaves early, without it. But we have a roach problem, right? In comes the exterminator at like 5:30. He needs to fumigate on a Friday night to give the office time to air out. He starts off in the kitchen, closing its doors. He sprays his pesticide all around the office as we clear out for the weekend. No one, I guess especially me, thinks to take the box home or whatever. I mean, it's a completely forgettable box. We're too busy, we're always running around like beheaded chickens, with fifty million last minute things to do. Monday, we've already forgotten about the fumigation. Baxter's one slice into the cake. It's big and doughy and, I guess, absorbent. But it didn't occur to me at the time. If it had occurred to me, I would have said something." *I could have said something sooner.* "He eats another slice. There's a baby Jesus inside."

"Wait, what?"

"A little plastic baby Jesus. That's what a King Cake is. It's supposed to be good luck." Binnie rubbed her face. "He chokes on the baby Jesus. I whack him on the back, but he's still choking and for some bizarre reason he runs to the bathroom. I follow him there and give him the Heimlich—"

"Why is this all news to me? You gave him the Heimlich? That's got to count for something!"

"I gave him the Heimlich. That's true." Still, she felt the violence of her gesture had been unwarranted. If she were fifty pounds heavier, she would have broken his ribs. A jagged rib bone piercing a lung. "I don't know. I'm obviously no doctor. But it set off a chain reaction, or maybe it just coincided with this horrible reaction to the pesticide. Vomit. Fever. The vomit was blue-green."

"Yes. I remember."

Her mouth was dry. "So I'm working late Wednesday night with Rick on this big oil case. And, I don't know, I get this *urge*. This need, all of a sudden to talk about it with someone who *knew* him—" She paused, glanced to the side, where a little mouse dropping sat beside the floorboard. *Hi*, the turd seemed to say. "He was listening to me so intently, Gary. He didn't really say anything." Her voice lowered. "He said, 'Listen, Binnie, just forget about it.' But, like, looked kind of smug and satisfied about it."

Gary leaned forward.

"And here's another weird thing that happened. I can't help but feel it's connected somehow. I found strange pictures on my computer. Scans of boudoir photos. Of Capra's girlfriend."

"I thought Capra was married."

"Well. There's this girl. Georgina. I meant to tell you." Gary's wholesomeness had put Binnie off from divulging this information. Salacious gossip seemed beneath him. Mostly she admired it, the wholesomeness. Mostly. "She came to the office once. Everyone just—accepted it."

"How come you're only telling me now?"

"I'm sorry—I don't know. I guess. I guess I thought you wouldn't be interested. It's just gossip."

"Huh."

"Anyway, I doubt Capra would be dumb enough or insane enough to put those pictures on my computer. I think someone is trying to mess with me. First I thought it was Rick. But maybe it's someone else. Like Capra's wife."

"Why would Capra's wife do that, though?"

"Because she's angry? Because she's never there and maybe thinks I'm Georgina?" Binnie hesitated. Capra's wife suspected Binnie of wrongdoing. Was Gary now suspicious too? "Listen, I think Rick's trying to get me fired. He's a sociopath! But, so. I tried something." She swallowed. "I told Capra about the photos and told him I feel extremely uncomfortable."

"Like harassment."

"Yeah, except I didn't use that word. Just implied it."

"What did he say?"

"He said all this is very complicated and that he would look into it. But see, I skipped something important. I was scared to say something about the boudoir photos sooner, because I didn't really want to pull Capra into this, I didn't believe he had anything to do with it. He's smarter than that. Anyway, at four o'clock today Capra pulls me into his office and says 'someone'—I think it was Rick but Capra wouldn't say—he said 'someone' has been saying I'm too careless and—do you think they can charge me with, like, man— " Her throat closed up again. Gary handed her a glass of water. "manslaugh-" She swallowed the water and unsteadily returned her glass to the table, hand shaking. "–ter?"

Softly, Gary asked, "Like for negligence?" She nodded, wished he hadn't asked that. "And you thought you could go to jail for something like that. So you threw in the pinups. Like a bargaining chip."

"I guess. Yeah. Plus the Heimlich." She rubbed her cheeks and eyes until she saw spots. Maybe he would be disgusted with how calculating she was. Break up with her. Turn her in, even. "But, Binnie. You weren't the only one aware of the pesticide, right? Isn't that on everyone?"

Binnie's voice got very small. She didn't look at Gary when she said, "I suppose so." She didn't want him to see the lie in her eyes. *Let them eat cake.*

"Okay. Okay." Gary took off his glasses and rubbed the bridge of his nose. His brow smoothed over. "Okay." He transformed into something else. Ultra Calm Man. "Maybe that helps you. Maybe not. Something's not gelling. Let's be on the safe side and assume it won't pan out. Maybe it would help if we do some research into manslaughter. Would that help?"

At first, the suggestion horrified her. He believed she was culpable and wanted her to get used to that idea. Then, she thought, maybe he meant something else. He had the same tendency she did to try to imagine the worst possible outcome, precisely so that it would never occur.

In bed, they hunched over Gary's laptop. The defense lawyer at the top of the search results specialized in accusations of rape and domestic abuse. "Let's pick someone else," Binnie said, sorely wanting another drink even as the room gently spun. Wikipedia listed varieties of manslaughter. She skipped down to the part about sentencing. For a lesser gross negligence, she could go away for three to 15 years. She pressed her face into a cushion and bellowed. Gary rubbed her back and said "Shhh, shhh, we'll figure this out."

Binnie wiped her eyes even as they kept streaming. "Maybe in prison I'll have time to make art? I'd be a real outsider then!" She laughed, somewhat crazed, and smashed her face into Gary's chest while he balanced the laptop on his knees and kept reading and saying *shhhh*. She accidentally yanked out some of his chest hairs as she gnashed her teeth. He said, "Ow! Get a hold of yourself, please!" Then *shhh, shhhh*.

Gary researched for what seemed like hours. *I think it'll be okay*, he said before putting away his laptop, *there's a lot that would need to be proved*. But the words barely penetrated her consciousness. She couldn't sleep. Baxter was *dead*.

At four in the morning, Binnie rose, careful not to wake Gary. The mattress creaked as she knelt by the window, which was really just an airshaft, illuminated indirectly by a street lamp. Opening it enough to peek out, she spied forms below: the faint outlines of discarded tricycles, deflated beach balls, and plastic dolls in the toy store's informal dump. Everything speckled with crumbled plaster. Cornell was down there, she imagined, knee-deep in junk, frantically salvaging. His body bent, viridescent moonlight on his fragile white hair. His breathing anxious. White grit scratching his fingertips. He unearthed a glass eyeball, cracked.

❖ ❖ ❖

Binnie's phone chirped. Gray light seeped through the window. It felt like she'd slept deeply for only twenty minutes or so. She curled into a fetal position, stretching her neck and lower back. Groaned. The phone chirped again. It was ten o'clock.

*Brunch? Want to come to Brooklyn?*
Ellen.

Her mind felt porous, her muscles clenched. She remembered what had happened and bolted upright, whole body in a primal state of alertness.

Gary turned in the sheets, snaking an arm around her waist.

"Want to get brunch with Ellen?"

He smacked his lips. His voice croaked as he said, "Seriously? Okay."

❖ ❖ ❖

In a sun-dappled corner of the restaurant's patio, tall potted ferns and orchids surrounded Ellen. She was reading *Art Forum*; the cover featured a black-and-white photo of iron crossbeams and planks of wood in disarray. Construction or destruction, it was hard to say.

"The mister sends his regrets," Ellen said, tucking the magazine into a leather bowling bag. Their metal chairs scraped on the terra cotta tile. The orchids' scent assaulted the nose: camphor and musky honey and artificial orange sweetener. It made Binnie think of cough drops and laryngitis.

The waitress asked, "Pitcher of mimosas?"

"Yes, please," all three replied.

Ellen and the waitress cackled. Binnie relaxed into her chair and snatched up a menu. If you were personable, she thought, you could make an okay living as a waitress. But you're probably looking at $3 an hour plus tips.

"Soooo, what's new?" Ellen asked in a singsong voice.

Binnie glanced at Gary; his face was a hazy tangle of meaning.

"Oh my god." Ellen's eyes sparkled as she leaned in. "Already?"

"What do you mean *already*?" Gary asked.

"Oh. You're not getting married?"

"No," said Gary.

Binnie blushed, Ellen's assumption and Gary's swift denial a bruise.

"You're *pregnant*?"

"No. Sorry to disappoint," Binnie mumbled.

"Oh, thank god." Her face bent toward the menu as she said, "No one should marry before thirty-five. It's like...running for Senate." The waitress reappeared holding a silvery pitcher wet with condensation and poured the first round of mimosas. Binnie drained half her flute in one gulp. Ellen watched her. "Mama's thirsty."

"Well, I might lose my job," she blurted.

Ellen closed her menu with a *thwap*. "No! What happened?" Talking amid the din of brunch seemed safe. Binnie told the story quietly. Gary listened, fidgeting with his napkin. Ellen snorted at the mention of the photographs. The hot, sickly sweet room combined with mimosas and Binnie's empty stomach worked quickly.

"But, Binnie," Ellen said, refilling her flute. "Did you *know* about the roach poison?"

"Well—sort of."

Ellen glanced at Gary, uncomfortable. Gary met her stare. Ellen inhaled, then waved her hand. "Come on. You couldn't have known."

Binnie recalled all the late-night conversations with Ellen where she'd dreamed up violent revenge art, like putting a man's plastic head on a spike, and felt herself shriveling. Was Ellen remembering those ideas? Was she saying *you couldn't have known* to protect her?

"And what about the photos?"

"What about them?"

"I mean, what do you think?"

"Sure, they're a problem, but not for you, exactly?"

Gary still wasn't saying anything. Why wasn't he saying anything? It dawned on Binnie what was happening. When people disappointed Gary, he dropped them. He dropped them and he would drop her, and maybe Ellen would be no better. She'd ripped out his chest hair, for crying out loud.

She shook her head. Stay. Rational.

And yet. She was standing.

"I'm not feeling so hot. I—I think I better go clear my head." The seat fell behind her with a head-throbbing clank. Yanking it upright, she headed for the door.

"Binnie, wait," Ellen said. The hot plastic curtain yielded.

"Binnie," said Gary.

"Maybe she needs some time to herself." The plastic muffled Ellen's words. The cold air between patio and restaurant was a brief reprieve. In the dim hall beside the restrooms, the "Black Hole" diorama re-emerged, except now instead of the roof of a Beaux Art bank caving in it was Binnie's head, and the expressionless, suited doll that had stood on the stone steps was inside her skull, and it was Baxter, with cake smeared around his mouth—or red donut jelly, or blood.

The door swung again, another burst of cold. Gary grabbed her arm. "Look, you need to try and be level-headed. Maybe today is not the day. But tomorrow it ought to be."

"Do you think they ever have muffins in jail?"

"Binnie, *stop*."

"Rikers smelled like ammonia and baloney."

"Listen, I did a lot of reading last night, and I think you're going to be okay. I don't think that's where all this is going."

"You're not a lawyer though! I appreciate it Gary, I do, but I don't think Wikipedia is going to make me feel better."

"Okay, I don't know, Binnie. I'm trying." His eyes narrowed in a way she'd never seen. "Go ahead," he said, voice flat and dry. "Hire a lawyer."

"I'm sorry." Her sensible leather loafers were starting to crack. She addressed her feet, frightened now that losing him felt imminent. "I didn't mean to snap."

"I know you're upset. And tired. I know *I'm* really tired."

The desire to talk to him caught in her throat. A stifled sensation between chest and tongue. "I'm—going to get out of your hair today. Can you tell Ellen I'm sorry for leaving?" She kissed him, a short sweet kiss. He held her other arm as she did.

"I'm worried about you," he murmured. Their eyes met soberly, a moment that felt real. Not a flirtation, not a performance, but something alive.

"I know," she said.

"Do you want me to come with you?"

"I—I'm not going do anything rash. I need to be by myself."

He nodded, reluctantly, scrutinizing her before she turned away.

❖ ❖ ❖

A noxious ball of anxiety somersaulted in her belly. Hire a lawyer? She could barely meet next month's rent! At Grand Army Plaza, she boarded the 2 train with no destination in mind. She felt like she was seeing things but flying blind. Her body jolted as the train whooshed toward Manhattan. The whoosh was what she wanted. The feeling of progress. Even if she wasn't fired, she realized, she probably couldn't stay at CZB. Not comfortably. Rick wins either way. What a scam. How could the pattern of quitting and firing be so obvious to her but go unmentioned by others? Perhaps because it didn't concern them, it wasn't their job at stake. It had been so *easy* to get the job, maybe that was the problem. 4.0? Low desired salary? Sure, we'll give you a spin.

Fuck Rick and his villainous cackle. He didn't exactly twirl a long mustache or rub his hands together while she lay on the train tracks all tied in a rope. But he wasn't a good person. Maybe he thought he was doing the right thing. Careless? Sure, she was careless. So careless she'd let someone eat cake!

Times Square was where she landed. The journey out of the subterranean air and through the clog of tourists halted, momentarily, the train of thought. She drifted to Bryant Park, the setting for Cornell's short film *Nymphlight*. Was he what she was after today? A trip back in time? A young Grace Kelly look-alike in white gossamer, carrying a broken parasol, sprints through a flock of pigeons. Tracks their upward flight to sky through fountain spray and canopy of trees. She disappears; green buses barrel down Forty-Second Street; there's a taste of 1957, men in white t-shirts, slicked hair, tight jeans. An elderly man in a blazer and red t-shirt slouches on a bench. The gossamer woman reappears, gazing at a girl in a blue skirt, lost yet apparently not distressed, twiddling with a button on her waist. The young woman's parasol ends up in the trash. The film ends with a dark reflection: a fountain grotesque—a sad old man in profile, a stand-in for Cornell—drips water into the pool, which ripples.

She began a pilgrimage to Cornell's old haunts, chewing on stale soft pretzel along the mile-and-half walk south. She imagined flipping through stacks of $1 ephemera at the cheap Fourth Avenue bookstalls, now long gone—collecting things. A photo of a film noir starlet with a cigarette perched on her pouty scarlet lip. Inspiration. She would sing a Gilbert & Sullivan operetta—*What, never? No, never!*—and the song would echo across an astronomical map from the Renaissance: visions of Galileo, Copernicus. Unpeeling these clues, imaginary gifts from the universe, her mind moved laterally, sifting for a creative solution.

What about the Bickford's, the Neddick's, the Woolworth's where Joseph ate jelly and custard cream and jotted notes about girls? The Strand Food Shop, where he met a waitress, Joyce Hunter, whose frequent presence in the Cornell home irked his mother. Who later stole his art for cash. Whom he forgave and bailed out and later gave more money. Who was murdered in her Upper West Side hotel home.

Was that her destiny? Death in an SRO?

Binnie's phone warmed in her fist; she was ready to pick up at its first vibration. Every few blocks, she checked the screen, and every few blocks there were no missed calls. She texted Gary, *thank you for everything* <3. The heart emoticon fell far short of what it was meant to do. When Gary didn't write back immediately she turned off her phone. Still southbound, she started seeing NYU dorms and swung east to Alphabet City. The forward motion, she hoped, would allow a plan to form, magically. But it didn't. The curiosity shop where she'd splurged on taxidermied sparrows was shut. (Had that been where she was heading all along?) A purple neon palm in a neighboring window offered $5 psychic readings. The woman inside, sly-eyed, beckoned Binnie with a finger. Binnie's shoulders hunched up. She turned her phone back on. and kept walking.

At three o'clock, just as she slipped into a dive bar, her phone rang and Capra's voice surprised her. *Kerblam* went her heart. She ran outside, plugged her free ear with a finger. Squinted at the slender trunk of a sidewalk tree in concentration.

"Listen, Binnie, I hope you're not too shaken up. Have you talked to a lawyer?"

"Not yet."

"Okay. Good. Can you come in tomorrow at eleven to meet with Mark and me?"

"Sure, of course."

"Meet us in the lobby."

"Sure, sure."

He hung up. Too quick to agree. Instead of a beer, she crossed the street for a $5 peanut butter and strawberry jelly milkshake. The kind of thing Joseph Cornell would lunch on, if there had been such an invention in his time. It was difficult to slurp the goop through her straw. The sludge sank into her belly.

❖ ❖ ❖

Anemic yellow light sifted through the Lipstick Building's lobby Sunday morning. Binnie waited by the shuttered newsstand. The security guard at the main desk scrolled through his phone. Zaiman and Capra arrived together; they buzzed her through the security gate.

"Did you have breakfast?" Zaiman asked, filling the silence.

"Yes." The rest of the elevator ride up was quiet; Capra's nose whistled.

They settled into Capra's office. Zaiman sat behind him on the edge of the credenza. At his back was the window looking down on 54th Street. The only thing visible was the glass and steel across the street.

"So here's the deal," Capra said, clearing his throat. "First I'd like to remind you of the NDA you signed when you started working here."

Binnie gulped. "Yes?"

"This is all highly confidential, you understand. But I'm telling you in case it brings you some peace of mind, some closure. As you recall, Kim objected to an autopsy on religious grounds."

"Yes."

"It would desecrate the body," Zaiman said.

"I'm sure she knows that," Capra said.

"It's worth mentioning."

Binnie hedged. "I thought she was Catholic?"

"In any case," said Zaiman. "Baxter wanted a Jewish burial. And time was getting on. The funeral was yesterday. A small, quiet ceremony."

"Oh. So...?" *A good lawyer knows the law. A great lawyer knows the judge.*

"So case closed," Capra said.

"And the—the negligence?"

" Who said anything about negligence?"

"Oh—I thought—I mean, didn't Rick imply—"

Capra long-blinked. "Let's set Rick aside for a moment. You'll be relieved to know that criminal negligence

would be a lot to prove and without Kim there's nothing doing. She wants to move on." Binnie sat back and
exhaled. A weight began to ever so slightly lift. "But, uh,
we do still need to have a discussion about your future.
About what's *best.*"

"What's best."

"You're not happy here, Binnie, and unfortunately
you let it show in your work. Times are tough, but we're
sure you'll find a great job. We're prepared to offer a
generous severance. And of course you can apply for
unemployment."

"*What*? What about the pictures? Is this about the
pictures?"

Zaiman asked, "What pictures?"

"On my computer. I told Mr. Capra on Friday. Naked
photos of Georgina, scanned to my desktop."

Zaiman grimaced. "Show us," he said, voice level. It
was like the grimace wasn't from shock but from embar-
rassment that Binnie would even pursue the issue at this
point.

They loomed over her at her computer, a cloud of
Old Spice and Ben Gay. She checked the email folder, the
Paralegal folder, the trash. She searched the whole hard
drive but it was excruciatingly slow. Capra's nose whis-
tled again and it sounded angry now. Once, he had joked,
"Your cheap boss should buy you a new computer," and
Beatrice had suggested she should give the tower a hearty
kick.

No images appeared. It had all been scrubbed.

"The pictures were *here*. I'm positive."

"Look, I think you're getting very mixed up and emotional," Capra said.

"Take the time off," Zaiman said. "A clean slate."

Binnie stared at the search box on her screen: zero files found.

"A generous severance," she said.

Capra softened. "Yes."

"I thought times were tough. Did this come out of Baxter's extra policy rider?"

"What are you—" Capra's lips pursed, making each word a dart.

"The one naming the firm as a beneficiary in case of his death."

Zaiman said urgently, volume rising, "Do you not see a good deal when it comes to you on a silver platter?"

Capra spoke firmly—quietly, eerily calm. "One month's pay."

Binnie found herself back at her interview, wondering if she'd asked for a high enough salary. She had no idea what constituted a "generous severance," but now seemed like the wrong time to dig in her heels. She remembered when Capra had laughed at a summary judgment, as if he'd gotten away with something scot-free. Her mouth twitched.

At the twitch, he added, "You've been here less than a year. Most people get one week's pay per year worked."

She rose. She looked neither of them in the eye. *Get out of here*, she thought. *Just get out.*

"Okay," she said.

"Very good," Capra answered. He returned to his

office. Zaiman and Binnie followed. Capra pushed a short document across the desk, referring to the NDA and the severance, and a windowed envelope with a check ready to go. Beatrice was in on it, Binnie assumed.

Zaiman handed her a pen.

"Well." She uncapped the pen.

"Atta girl," Zaiman said quietly as she signed.

The flying goat on the Chagall print by the door brayed. Her stomach squirmed.

"Settlement": a cedar box of dirt filled with worms. The viewer may add soil atop them and tamp them down, but the worms persist, wriggling up, slimy against the viewer's palms.

❖ ❖ ❖

That night she found herself back in Kensington, bawling and hiccupping with her head in her mother's lap. Arlene stroked her head.

"Maybe it is for the best."

The worms of "Settlement" writhed.

Albert patted her head, said *there, there*, and steeped a concoction of Sleepy Time Extra and Tension Tamer tea. Added a big squirt of honey. They opened up the couch and tucked her in with an old comforter. A *Wheel of Fortune* marathon washed her in a rainbow swirl.

The next day, while Arlene went to work, Binnie and Albert walked to the bank on Park Circle to deposit the check.

"Maybe...I could get a job in your shop?" she asked. Hacking wood all day wouldn't be so bad.

He did not wave his pinkie stump in disapproval. "Maybe." His lower lip turned. "Take some time to think."

❖ ❖ ❖

Albert went on to his shop. On Prospect Park West, a new café had opened, the nearest place that wasn't a greasy spoon. Alone, Binnie shivered on the edge of one of the freshly painted Adirondack chairs outside. They sat in a sprightly row of red, white, and blue. The café had a stupid name: The Boonies. But it was perhaps appropriate, given the cell reception at her parents' place. She flipped open her phone and dialed a number anyway. Across the street, Canadian geese lurched over the treetops, honking in syncopation.

"This is Alexis."

"Oh, hi. Um. This is Binnie Greenson?"

"Who?"

"Binnie. Binnie Greenson. We spoke just after New Year's. You saw a diorama of mine and said to call."

"Oh?"

"I left you a message a while back. I'm sure you're very busy, so I thought I'd give you another ring."

A breath. "Help me out here."

"The little boy and the marigolds?"

"Yes! Right. Charming." Cars whooshed by. "Tell me more about your work."

An ambulance siren made her cringe.

"Well, uh—" She hadn't had to talk about her work in a long time. "I like to do dreamy assemblages, but I've also played with silicone. My senior year show was a silicone cast of my foot." Why was she bringing that up? Her professor had liked the title, "Finding My Footing," but it had been so on the nose it was like a curse, and here she was and she still hadn't found her schtick. Gary was right. She needed to practice one. "I like to combine found objects to create a dreamlike narrative," she said. "I'm a big fan of Joseph Cornell? His ephemeral qualities." It was so jumbled. She was throwing anything out there, hoping something would stick.

"Oh, yes, yes. I can see that. You know, there was a lovely show—now I'm just thinking aloud, I'll have to go back and look. I'd make a terrible art historian, ha," she said, her speech cranking up in speed as she seemed to position Binnie in a certain slot. "I'm trying to remember who was in it. Jackson Pollock, I think. Pollock or someone of that stature in the front and an intimate room of Cornell's assemblages in the back. I might like to do something like that. The big and the intimate together. The intimate sort of a dark, warm...*cocoon*." Her voice resonated on the last word as if she dreamed of crawling inside it herself.

"Oh?" Binnie recalled something about that show. Cornell had felt slighted by the arrangement. Pushed into a corner. Still, she surged forward.

"Come by and show me a few more pieces," Alexis said. "Whatever you like. No promises, of course, but maybe we'll spark something." *Spark something* had a flirtatious ring to it. The sale of art a dance of seduction.

Her chest pounded. Her throat opened. Something to live for.

"Happy to. When?"

"Oh, any time, I suppose—uh-oh. I'm sorry, I gotta go. But do come by."

A few pieces. She bit her lip. Birth, sex, death. Birth, sex, death of childhood? The little plastic baby. The pinup. The altar to the ice cream smile.

❖ ❖ ❖

She put off texting Gary again. He would be happy for her, she was sure. But he hadn't texted. And she couldn't tell if he was giving her space or wanted it for himself. Preemptive protection. She would tell no one until she had something *real*.

At her work table she collected a Raggedy Andy doll, a toy gun, a John Wayne figurine; tiny plastic colts, tumbleweeds made for architectural models, and Monopoly money; credit card offers, foreclosure documents, pocket-sized Bibles, headlines from the *Wall Street Journal*; every distinct picture of Bernie Madoff's sorry face available in print; Mardi Gras beads and multi-colored sugar and little pink plastic baby Jesuses. She wanted to make things that turned off the analytical brain and tugged tongue and heart in opposite directions, but these were the objects she compulsively collected, the ones that made her feel like she had some minuscule bit of control. Obvious Statements. But that was what compelled.

In her fantasy world, if she'd made her Lipstick Building installation, one floor would be "Wild, Wild Wilmington" and encompass all of these objects: an avalanche of rogue cowboy businessmen, game show–style Mardi Gras hysteria, televangelist pyramid schemes, Madoff, Medici, slot machine cacophony, an unsettling soundscape of laugh tracks and mania, and, off in a dark corner, something less careful viewers might miss: a hunchbacked underworld god of jewels, a Quasimodo Pluto. A mixed metaphor monster, who wants to be loved, whom you want to love, but who must die. Skin (silicone?) erupting with dim emeralds and shining boils, chest subtly rising and falling with spasmodic wheezes.

❖ ❖ ❖

Googling prosthetic eyes again, she found something a bit more affordable than the $60 peepers she'd first found in November. She would see Alexis soon. Before Alexis forgot her again. Eighteen seemed like a lucky number to start with. She splurged on nine pairs, two-day delivery. Couldn't lose momentum now, could she?

# Chapter Fourteen

THE BOX OF EYEBALLS arrived on time. She still hadn't decided where to move, how far out she would have to go to keep things affordable. She read the rest of Yayoi Kusama's autobiography. Kusama was somewhat contrite about her meanness to Cornell but justified it by explaining how clingy and needy he had been. *Dalí picks me up in a Rolls Royce*, she said to him when he was recovering from prostate surgery and asked her to visit; *can't you show more respect for the love of your life?* It was a depressing anecdote. But the arrival of the eyeballs buoyed Binnie up.

She cut open the cardboard and lifted off the bubble wrap. Pupils-up, nestled in egg crates cushioned with paper shreds. A mix of blue, blue-grey, grey, green, brown, hazel, violet. She'd bought a springform cake pan. She set it on the floor and sat beside it with the box of eyes. In a circle, inside the pan, she laid out the tower's base: six balls, irises out. She nestled Olsen's shard in the middle.

The piece's special secret. Chewed on a green Mike n' Ike and contemplated this first tentative step. Nursed lime flavoring off a molar.

Problem was, she had to remove the cake pan structure to see the work clearly. What if it sucked? Yet gluing the balls together was too much of a commitment. She wanted to see what she was doing, but premature glue could ruin her investment. The adhesive could only go on after she knew it looked right. Conundrum!

She exhaled. Use your imagination, Binnie. You have to start somewhere. You have to take each step. She sniffed at a pink Mike n' Ike, held it on her tongue. Studied a laminated anatomical diagram, soaking up the names of eye parts she didn't know: choroid, fovea, optic disc, aqueous humor. Ideas to collect and ponder. She kept the first layer in the pan scaffold. Added five more eyes on top, the next level in the tower. Crystals of artificial strawberry expanded on her tongue.

The phone vibrated.

*How are you doing?*

Gary.

*So sorry I haven't been in touch*, she wrote. *It's been—tumultuous.*

*I'm sure. Meet me for dinner?*

Her heart surged, then sank. Was this his version of we need to talk?

*Anywhere you like, anytime. Lots of free time now.*

*You lost your job??*

*I'll tell you in person.*

*5:30? The Flushing Main Street station?*

*Can't wait. Miss you.*

An excruciating pause.

*Miss you too, Binnie.*

She surged at that. *He misses me.* In a bout of feeling good, in a bout of thinking *clearly*, she deconstructed the eyeball tower and discarded Olsen's eye shard. The pirate banker's eye had no place in her tower. It was, she thought, a relic of a rotten system and the relic need not be at the core of her piece.

Would that make any sense to her later? She delicately placed the eye shard in the waste basket that had held her rubber octopus and all manner of materials hoarded and discarded before the trial. She put the eyeballs back in the cake pan. But she couldn't bear to stay inside and work out a thorough solution just now, even though she had hours to kill.

She put a little sketch book in her purse and headed for a Queens-bound train; at the top of the stairs she stopped herself, having a better idea. Went east, to the 59th Street bridge, zoomed up in the gondola over the East River to Roosevelt Island, past the blackened ruins of the mental hospital where Nelly Bly had feigned insanity. In that report she'd written in middle school, that unit on great New Yorkers, the story of the cold baths had struck her: how the inmates had been "treated" with icy water. The island was called Blackwell's before being renamed Roosevelt. Names masking identity. Changing identity. Maybe she needed a new name. A persona.

What was Ruby's maternal grandmother's maiden name? What had she wanted? The usual: husband, children, health, happiness. As a newcomer, a nimble-fingered child in Brooklyn, she rolled paper flowers around wires for lady's hats. Her daughter became a seamstress. Her grand-daughter, Ruby, manned a perfume counter. What had Ruby dreamed? Snapdragons and gladiolas in a cut-glass vase graced her nightstand every day until she couldn't get to the florist down the street. Had the lack of flowers propelled her decline?

Binnie continued on to Queens.

Joseph Cornell had lived on Utopia Parkway. She knew he wasn't the answer to her problems, yet in some intangible way she needed to see where he'd lived, glimpse through a basement window the place where he'd worked for hours and hours alone. As if she would see his fragile, bird-like bones. The back of his neck, small, wrinkled, and vulnerable.

The idea of him was like a meditation stone she thumbed in her pocket. Despite the lurid gossip about him, he maintained an aura of innocence. He'd once made an art show for children, with chocolate sodas and artwork at eye-level for little ones. It was an idea that made her happy. It had perspective. In his biography, in the first pages, the author said that Cornell's childhood didn't teach him to meet the challenges of life but how to avoid them—that in order to survive, his life would need to be a profound act of imagination. That idea had stopped Binnie in her tracks. She wanted, and didn't want, to know more. She worried knowing more would ruin his art for her. But even as she learned more about him, read more about the private details of his life that he surely would not have wanted made public and the prurient insinuations on anonymous internet discussion boards, he continued on in her mind as a figure on which she meditated. Not as a goal. She did not want to live like him. But somehow a guide. She could not explain it.

The tract of land that became Utopia, Queens had been named by developers wanting to build real estate for Jewish families who moved up from the tenements of the Lower East Side in the late nineteenth century. The developers went bankrupt before they could build, so it remained farmland until the 1940s, when another developer, billing itself as "America's largest homebuilder," put up twenty-four blocks of two- and three-bedroom Cape Cods and Colonials. Cornell's family didn't settle into one of these developments because they'd already been living there; they lived in an older house on Utopia Parkway, having moved out of a rambling Victorian in Nyack. His mother, in Nyack, had been accustomed to the finer things. Trips to Hudson Valley resorts. Bridge parties. Lace doilies. Operettas. After becoming a widow and moving to Queens with Joseph and Robert, whom she'd considered a burden, she'd felt deeply bitter. This was not the life trajectory she'd hoped for.

The parkway ran north-south along the neighborhood's easternmost border. Binnie took a bus from the train in Kew Gardens, intending to stroll the length of the parkway. She had to give up the studio soon; maybe she'd move deep into Queens? She'd see if there was a plaque on Cornell's house, if it was landmarked, if she could divine anything from it, if it had a ghostly presence. She thought about meeting Gary, right when he got off work for the day. They could reconcile; they could travel the world together, one stop on the 7 train at a time. Or maybe over bulgogi he'd let her down gently, ruin Korean BBQ for her forever.

Her thoughts, her neuroses, tainted everything.

It amazed her that some people lived and worked in one borough their whole lives, maybe never even left that borough. Cornell in later years shrank his world, rarely leaving Queens, preferring the Flushing branch of the library to the stately central branch on Fifth Avenue where the reference librarians had shared with him their vast knowledge of the children's literature archives and invited him to display his work in the children's reading room. This one-borough existence was as common for residents of Bay Ridge, Brooklyn, as it was for many a Manhattanite who vowed to try and leave the island at least once a month and failed. There were so many tiny, self-contained universes. What was the cosmology of New York City? Which areas were dark stars, red dwarves? Which were now growing, pulsing with the strongest gravitational pull? Where would she be pulled? Would she find work in the Brooklyn Navy Yard? Could she find herself a nice black hole in which to disappear?

No plaque marked the building; it was not a historic landmark. Hesitating in front of the small green lawn, she approached the unassuming house, hoping whoever lived inside would not shoo her away. Sunset through the smog shone orange-fuschia against its white siding. She touched what had been the Cornell house, where Joseph had cared for his ailing brother and his nagging mother, where he survived them both and grieved their losses in "a nightmare of an empty house"; where he'd "subsisted on weak tea and store-bought cake"; where in the basement he'd spent countless hours alone, arranging and rearranging his collages and dream boxes, forever works-in-progress he could almost never let go.

The musty windows reflected pink light on Binnie. She glanced over her shoulder at the sun. Turned back to Cornell's house with a flare of light in her eye. The image of his house doubled and twisted in the air as her gaze moved up beyond its sloped rooftop toward the sky, as if it were a film projection refracted through a prism, a series of film stills overlapping, a mixed-up zoetrope, a three-dimensional eight-pointed star. The twisting house grew enormous in its multiplying, its overlapping corners forming facets like a cut-glass perfume bottle or a tower converted from steel and granite to pink rock candy, or thousands of shards of cracked glass eyes catching light.

Silvery wind chimes stirred on a neighboring porch. Dazzled, Binnie focused on the cool grass at her feet, the damp air a haze of twilit lavender. She thought of that botched senior project, her silicone foot, and contemplated the difference between silicone and skin. She slipped off her shoes and stood on the grass.

In her mind's eye, the storied house pulses, hovers, grows.

A gray dog barks from an open window on an upper floor, a powerful animal with warm eyes. Lacy white curtains drape his muscular head. She imagines the pleasant touch of soft eyelets on his fur, the way the fabric brushes the dog's skull, the way its draping seems maternal. She steps away from the house and waves, and the dog barks louder, hi— hi— hellooooooooooooo. Softly, she smiles. And the dog, hollering, raises up his snout to the paling disc of the sun.

## About the Author

ANCA L. SZILÁGYI is the author of the novel *Daughters of the Air*, which *Shelf Awareness* called "a striking debut from a writer to watch" and *The Seattle Review of Books* called "a creation of unearthly talents." Her writing appears in *Orion Magazine*, *Lilith Magazine*, and *Los Angeles Review of Books*, among other publications. She is the recipient of fellowships and awards from Hugo House, Jack Straw Cultural Center, 4Culture, Artist Trust, and Vermont Studio Center. Originally from Brooklyn, she has lived in Montreal, Seattle, and now Chicago, where she teaches creative writing and lives with her husband and son.

## Acknowledgments

I AM GRATEFUL for the many people who helped this book into existence. Thank you to Christine Neulieb, once again, for your brilliant editorial insights. Thank you kind, early readers of whole or partial drafts: Kris Waldherr, Larry Zuckerman, Corinne Manning, Nancy Jooyoun Kim, Kristen Millares Young, Sonora Jha, Lisa Nicholas, Paul Vega (rest in peace, dear friend), Peter Mountford, Lacey Clemmons, and Irene Keliher. And my 2015 Jack Straw Writers Program cohort, Linda Andrews, Emily Bedard, Laura Da', Bernard Grant, Clare Johnson, Martha Kreiner, Erin Malone, Ross McMeekin, L. J. Morin, Matthew Schnirman, and Jeanine Walker. Thanks to Bryan Edenfield for the Ekphrantics event at Greg Kucera Gallery, which generated Binnie's idea for the Lipstick Building art squat installation.

Thank you to 4Culture for supporting this novel with a 2014 Art Project Grant. Thank you to the Jack Straw Cultural Center, Levi Fuller, Joan Rabinowitz, and Kevin

Craft, 2015 Writers Program curator, for supporting this book.

Thank you to David Eaton and Sonia Cook for providing feedback on legal content in the book; any mistakes are, of course, mine.

Thank you to Amanda Thomas and Feliza Casano and everyone at Lanternfish Press for being such lovely, hard-working people.

Thank you, always, to my parents for encouraging my creative pursuits. Thank you, always, to Michael Podlasek Kent, for reading multiple drafts and supporting my endeavors. Thank you Judy Kent and Annabelle Barclay for help watching Damian so this novel could get done. Thank you Damian, sweet boy, for being enamored with lights and string.